DOCTOR WHO
THE SENSORITES

DOCTOR WHO
THE SENSORITES

Based on the BBC television series by Peter R. Newman by
arrangement with the British Broadcasting Corporation

NIGEL ROBINSON

Number 118 in the
Doctor Who Library

A TARGET BOOK

published by
the Paperback Division of
W. H. ALLEN & CO. PLC

A Target Book
Published in 1987
By the Paperback Division of
W. H. Allen & Co. PLC
44 Hill Street, London W1X 8LB

First published in Great Britain by
W. H. Allen & Co. PLC 1987

The BBC producers of *The Sensorites* were Verity Lambert
and Mervyn Pinfield, the directors were Mervyn Pinfield
and Frank Cox

The role of the Doctor was played by William Hartnell

Printed and bound in Great Britain by
Anchor Brendon Ltd, Tiptree, Essex

ISBN 0 426 20295 3

Contents

Prologue

Out in the still and infinite blackness of uncharted space, hundreds of light years from its planet of origin, the spacecraft hung, caught like a fly in a gigantic spider's web. Here in the outermost reaches of the galaxy few stars shone; what little illumination there was came from the bright yellow world around which the ship moved in perpetual orbit, and that planet's mother star.

If there had been human eyes to watch, they would have recognised the ship as an interplanetary survey vessel, one of many sent out from its home planet in the early years of the twenty-eighth century to search for new sources of minerals to replace those long since squandered on Earth. Nearly a fifth of a mile in length and with its dull grey hull studded with innumerable scars, the result of thousands of meteor storms encountered in its four year journey, its survey had been almost complete when it entered this region of the galaxy; and now here it remained, a ghost-like satellite in the planet's otherwise moonless sky.

Along the cold and empty corridors of the ship all was still, save for the occasional tinkling of an on-board computer and the steady rhythmic pulse of the life support system. Otherwise a ghastly silence reigned, as impenetrable as stone and as quiet as the dark and lonely grave.

The crew's quarters, the recreational areas, even the power rooms and laboratories were also empty and shrouded in semi-darkness. All unnecessary power had long since been reduced automatically to a minimum: where there were no living creatures there was also no need for light.

Upon the flight deck, once the hub of all activity on board the spaceship, the same all pervasive stillness was supreme. By the navigation and command consoles, their forms half-hidden in the baleful light of the scanners, sat two motionless figures – a man and a woman. Dressed in the same one-piece military grey tunics, they were slumped over their respective control boards, their ashen faces totally oblivious of their surroundings, or of the digital read-outs displayed on the computer screens above their heads.

A single blinking light on a control console indicated that the ship was in flight, continuing its interminable and purposeless orbit of the yellow planet. But there was no one on board the ship able to acknowledge its futile warning, nor to take any action to alter the spaceship's course.

To all intents and purposes, it was a ship of dead men, going nowhere.

1

Strangers in Space

In the dazzling expansive surroundings of a control room which boasted instruments no one on twenty-eighth century Earth could even have dreamed of, the four people around the central control console seemed strangely out of place. As out of place, in fact, as the antique bric-à-brac which crowded the room.

The youngest of the four was a teenager, dressed in the style of clothes common to Earth in the 1960s. No longer a girl, and not yet quite a woman, her closely cropped hair framed a face of almost Asiatic prettiness, and her dark almond eyes belied an intelligence far beyond her tender years. Her companions were all turned intently towards the flickering instrumentation on one of the six control panels of the central console. She, however, looked enquiringly at the puzzled face of the silver-haired old man, from whose side she seldom strayed and whom she trusted implicitly.

'What is it, Grandfather? What's happened to the TARDIS?' she asked, her tone wavering as she tried hard to conceal the inexplicable sense of unease she felt within herself.

The old man looked up. 'I really don't know, my child, I really don't know,' he said, tapping the fingers of his blue-veined hands together as was his habit when faced with a vexing problem.

He wore a long Edwardian frock coat, checked trousers, a crisp wing-collar shirt and a meticulously tied cravat. He seemed every bit the image of a well-bred English gentleman of leisure rather than the captain of a highly advanced time and space machine.

Turning to his other companions he drew their attention to the tall glass column which now rested motionless in the centre of the hexagonal control console. 'All indications are that the TARDIS has materialised. But that' – and here he pointed to one persistently flashing light on the control board – 'says we are still moving. Now, what do you make of that, hmm?'

The third member of the TARDIS crew spoke up, a tall tidy woman in her late twenties, with a stern purposeful face which nevertheless possessed a melancholy beauty. Like Susan she too dressed in the fashion of late twentieth-century Earth, though her more conservative clothes reflected her maturer years. 'Perhaps we've landed *inside* something?' she suggested. 'Perhaps that's why we appear to be moving? What do you think, Ian?'

'You could be right, Barbara,' agreed the stocky well-built young man beside her. He spoke to the old man: 'Try the scanner again, Doctor; let's see what's outside.'

The Doctor activated a switch and the four travellers looked up at the scanner screen, set high in one of the roundelled walls of the control room. The picture on the screen was nothing but a blanket of random flashes and lines.

'Covered with static,' observed the Doctor.

'That could be caused by a strong magnetic field,' Ian ventured.

'Yes. Or an unsuppressed motor,' agreed his older companion.

'Can we go outside, Grandfather?' asked Susan.

The Doctor allowed himself a small smile, recognising in his granddaughter the same insatiable curiosity which had caused them to begin their travels so very long ago. He nodded his assent: 'I shan't be satisfied till we've solved this little mystery.'

By his side, Barbara sighed. 'I don't know why we bother to leave the TARDIS sometimes,' she said gloomily.

'You're still thinking about your experiences with the Aztecs,' remarked the Doctor.

Barbara's mouth formed a rueful half-smile. 'No, I've got over that now,' she said, recalling a previous adventure in fifteenth-century Mexico. There she had unsuccessfully attempted to put to an end the Aztecs' barbaric practice of human sacrifice. The Doctor had watched her struggle with wry admiration, knowing all the time that no mortal man could ever halt the irreversible tide of history. The Aztecs *had* practised human sacrifice and nothing that Barbara or even he – travellers out of time – could do would ever alter that immutable historical fact. The Doctor had long ago come to terms with the futility of attempting to change history, but Barbara could never stand back and watch her fellow creatures suffer. Cold scientific observation was all very well, but it meant nothing if not tempered with human compassion and love.

But she would eventually accept the strictures placed on travellers in the fourth dimension, thought the Doctor. Yes, Barbara and Ian would learn from their fellow travellers, just as he and Susan would learn from them.

The Doctor paused for a moment to recall his first meeting with Ian and Barbara. Teachers at Coal Hill School in the London of 1963 and curious about the background of their most baffling pupil, they had followed Susan one foggy night to an old scrapyard in a shadowy road called Totters Lane. There they had finally met the girl's grandfather and guardian – an intellectual giant known only as the Doctor, an alien cut off from his home planet by a million light years in space and thousands of years in time. And there too they had stumbled across the secret of the TARDIS – a craft of infinite size, capable of crossing the dimensions of time and space, and housed in the impossible confines of a battered old police telephone box.

Originally unwilling fellow travellers, Ian and Barbara had grown fond of their alien companions, as had the Doctor and Susan of them. And though at times the two teachers – Barbara especially – thought longingly of returning to their own planet, their journeys through time and space still inspired in them a great pioneering spirit; what had started so long ago as a mild curiosity in a junkyard had now turned into quite an exciting adventure.

The Doctor applied himself once more to the problem in hand. With an experience born of countless journeys, his eyes dashed quickly over the dials and digital displays on the console. Satisfied with the read-outs from the TARDIS computer, he turned to his granddaughter. 'Open the doors, Susan,' he commanded.

'You've checked everything then, Doctor?' asked Ian.

'Of course I have, Chesterton,' he replied peevishly. 'Plenty of oxygen and the temperature's quite normal.'

'So there's just the unknown then,' said Barbara.

'Precisely!'

Susan operated a small control on the console. With a gentle hum the great double doors opened. All four travellers felt the same thrill of anticipation they always felt upon entering a new world. What would lay waiting for them beyond the doors?

The police box exterior of the TARDIS had materialised inside a long shadowy corridor. But for the large circular doors which periodically interrupted the ridged aluminium panelling of the walls, the time-machine might just as easily have landed in an underground tunnel: everywhere there was the same claustrophobic sense of doom and menace. Indeed, the air seemed as stale and musty as the air of any tunnel could. There was no sound to be heard.

'You were right, Barbara,' said Ian; 'we have landed inside something.'

'It's a spaceship!' exclaimed the Doctor triumphantly, satisfied now that the mystery of the TARDIS's apparent motion had been explained. 'Close the doors, Susan,' he said to his granddaughter, and then addressed his other companions: 'Let us be careful: there seems to have been some sort of catastrophe here.'

With the TARDIS doors securely locked, the crew ventured cautiously down the spacecraft's grey corridor. The design of the ship seemed to be solely functional and was devoid of any decoration or colour. Whoever the ship's crew might be, thought Barbara, they must be very dreary – or extremely dedicated. But as she walked down the long passageway, almost wading though the oppressive silence, she began to wonder if the ship was inhabited at all; perhaps it had been abandoned years ago, left to drift through all eternity like a *Mary Celeste* of space?

The Doctor had considered it wise to keep to one corridor, rather than pursue any of the connecting passageways or doors, and after some minutes the four friends came upon what they took to be the spaceship's main flight deck. Here the gloom was dispersed somewhat by the illuminated screens set around the walls, and the view of a bright yellow planet through the observation port. Several banks of computers lined the walls and they chattered away spasmodically to each other. But other than that the place was dead: no movement, no life, nothing.

It was Ian who first saw the two bodies. Rushing over to the man, he raised his head from where it had slumped onto the control panel, and felt for a pulse. Nothing. Shaking his head, he returned to the others, one heavy word on his lips: 'Dead.'

'Look, this one's a girl,' cried Susan, going over to the body at the navigation console.

Barbara quickly joined her and, like Ian, checked for signs of life. 'I'm afraid she's the same,' she sighed. 'What could have happened to them? I can't see a wound or anything.'

'Suffocation, Doctor?' ventured Ian.

'I never make uninformed guesses, my friend,' said the Doctor, tapping his coat lapels, 'but that's certainly one possibility.' He looked down at the dead girl's face. Her fair hair was piled in disarray on top of her head, but there was still a prim beauty about her. 'Such a great tragedy. She's only a few years older than Susan.'

While her companions had been examining the bodies, Susan had stood back, feeling once again that strange sense of unease she had experienced before in the TARDIS. It wasn't the fact that these two young astronauts were dead; she had seen death before, in many gruesome forms. But this was something different, *inexplicable*. It was as if a thousand voices were shouting in her head, telling her to get off this ship of dead men while she still had the chance. 'Grandfather, let's get back to the TARDIS. Please . . .' Her voice trembled.

'Why, my child?' asked the Doctor, looking up from the dead girl's face.

'I . . . I don't know. I've got a . . . *feeling* . . . about this . . .'

Barbara moved closer to her erstwhile pupil. 'Yes, I can feel something too . . .'

Hardly a great respecter of female intuition, even Ian had

to admit that there was something distinctly unnerving about this dark and silent ship. 'You mean whatever killed them could kill us too?'

Even if Barbara and Susan could have explained their irrational fears the Doctor left them no time to answer. In an attempt to determine the cause of death, he had been examining the young girl and pointed out to Ian the watch she was wearing. 'Chesterton, do you notice anything unusual about this watch?' he asked.

Ian shook his head in bewilderment.

The Doctor continued: 'It isn't working. Now, this model is one of the old automatic types: it depends on the movement of the wrist to recharge the spring inside every twenty-four hours.'

Ian looked at the time displayed on the watch. 'And it's stopped at three o'clock,' he observed.

'Then if we say that it's just stopped, that would mean that the last movement of this poor child's wrist would be twenty-four hours ago.'

'That's all very well, Doctor,' Barbara said practically, 'but it still doesn't tell us anything about how they died.'

The Doctor shrugged his shoulders. It was his habit to seek out every possible piece of information. But even he had to admit that in this particular case his findings had helped very little.

Susan had meanwhile moved over to the dead man and idly lifted his wrist to look at his watch. Suddenly she let out a little scream of shock, dropping the man's limp arm. 'Grandfather! He's *warm*!'

Barbara rushed over. 'Then this one's just died!'

'But look at his watch, Barbara,' said Ian. 'It's stopped at three o'clock too.'

'It doesn't make sense, does it?' said the Doctor, evaluating the situation. 'But all the facts are here before us: the watches stopped at least twenty-four hours ago, but we know that this poor fellow's just died. Now, why should that be, hmm?'

He looked challengingly at his companions, who returned his look with blank faces. Here was another mystery for the Doctor to solve, another solution to seek out, but . . . Like his three friends before him, the Doctor felt the icy hand of

14

uncertain fear touch him. Perhaps it might be better to let the dead rest in peace . . . He shook his head: 'I think it would be wise if we returned to the Ship, and leave these people. There's nothing we can do for them.'

Ian, Barbara and Susan breathed an almost audible communal sigh of relief. At last they would leave this place of irrational fear and unknown menace and return to the bright security of the TARDIS.

'We can't even bury them,' sighed Barbara.

'Come along then, let's get back to the TARDIS,' the Doctor urged.

The four walked slowly back to the entrance to the corridor. Allowing themselves one last look at the sad scene on the flight deck they turned – to see the dead man fall forward onto his control panel, and to hear him give out a long groan of anguish.

Ian bounded over to him, shaking by the shoulders what had but a minute ago been a corpse. Now the man's eyelids were fluttering, and his gaunt swarthy features were contorted in pain.

'His heart had stopped beating, Doctor!' Ian protested. '*He was dead!*'

Not only was he now alive but his parched lips were also moving. Ian bent down to him in an attempt to hear the words he was struggling to say. With one painful move of his arm, the once-dead man indicated a shelving unit at the far end of the flight deck.

Ian went over to the unit. 'What is it? What do you want?' he asked as he searched the contents of the shelves. His hands alighted on a small box-like device. 'Is this what you want?'

From the man's lips came a croak of affirmation. Ian rushed back to him, and he grabbed the device with a surprising vigour, clutching it almost possessively to his chest.

Within a matter of seconds, the colour had returned to the man's deathly pale complexion, and he was able to sit upright in his chair. He rubbed his eyes in an attempt to refocus his vision and then handed the box over to Barbara and nodded towards his colleague. 'Place this against Carol's chest,' he said, his voice still barely more than a whisper.

Barbara looked down at him with pity. 'I'm sorry, Carol's

15

dead.'

'*Please do as I ask!*'

Resigned, Barbara did as instructed. As with the man it took but a few seconds for the girl to revive and sit up. She looked around her in confusion until Barbara's friendly smiling face allayed her fears.

'But you were both dead,' Ian maintained. 'What was in that box?'

'It's a heart resuscitator,' the man explained to the baffled schoolteacher. His voice was rapidly becoming steadier and stronger. 'When you found us we were in a very long sleep. Most of our vital functions had been suspended – but we weren't dead.'

With a little help from Barbara the girl called Carol came over to the man who introduced himself to the time-travellers. 'My name is Maitland. This is Carol Richmond, my co-astronaut.'

'We're pleased to meet you,' said Ian and introduced his party to the astronauts.

'Tell me, young man,' began the Doctor, 'are you from Earth?'

Maitland nodded.

'How's it looking then?' asked Barbara cheerily, suddenly realising that Maitland and Carol were the first near-contemporaries she and Ian had met since they began their travels with the Doctor.

'There's still too much air traffic,' Carol replied wryly.

'They got it off the roads then, did they?' was Ian's rejoinder. Like Barbara he had quickly warmed to the two astronauts. 'We come from London,' he offered. 'Tell me, is Big Ben still on time?'

'Big Ben? What's that?' asked Carol.

'It's a clock near Westminster Abbey,' Barbara explained.

Maitland attempted to enlighten her. 'The whole lower half of London is now called Central City,' he said. 'There hasn't been a London for over four hundred years.'

Barbara and Ian exchanged a look of astonishment as Maitland continued: 'This is the twenty-eighth century. Which century do you come from? The twenty-first perhaps?'

Before the development of hyper space travel, it had become customary to put astronauts in cryogenic suspension, so that they would sleep the long journey to their destination. With the establishment of hyper space travel it was becoming increasingly common for astronauts to actually overtake spaceships which might have left Earth generations before using conventional power sources. Maitland had quite naturally assumed that the Doctor's party were astronauts from an early age who had been reawakened from their suspended animation and come aboard his ship.

Carol interrupted Ian and Barbara's hesitant explanations. 'Captain Maitland, these people must leave us immediately.' There was a quiet determination in her voice of which both Barbara and Ian were acutely aware.

'Yes,' agreed Maitland, 'you can't stay here.'

'Why not?' protested Ian. 'There are so many things we want to learn.'

'No. There's danger here. You must go.' The tone was final.

'Danger?' asked Barbara, her senses alerted. 'What sort of danger?'

Maitland shook his head. 'It's better you don't know what happened to us . . .'

'But we might be able to help,' she insisted.

The Doctor had been listening to this conversation with increasing interest and interrupted his companion. 'No, Barbara, I learnt not to meddle in other people's lives years ago,' he chided her.

Ian instantly snorted with disbelief, as though Attila the Hun had just declared that all he wanted to do was stay at home and look after the children. The Doctor did not fail to notice this.

'Now, don't be absurd!' he snapped. 'There's not an ounce of curiosity in me, my dear boy!' Ignoring Ian and Barbara's chuckles of derision, he asked Maitland, 'Tell me – *why* are you in danger?'

There was something in the Doctor's eager searching eyes which made Maitland realise the utter futility of dissuading the old man now that his curiosity had been aroused.

'Very well, I'll try to explain,' he said and pointed to the view port near the navigation console. Framed in the port was a bright yellow planet. 'Out there is what we call the Sense-Sphere. Its inhabitants – the Sensorites – have always prevented us from leaving this area of space.'

'You mean that they have some sort of power over your spacecraft, keeping it in orbit around their planet?' asked the Doctor.

'It's not quite that simple. They not only control our craft, they also have some sort of influence over us.'

'Hypnosis?'

Maitland shook his head and the Doctor pressed him further.

'They have some sort of control over our brains,' Maitland said. 'These Sensorites are hostile but in the strangest possible way: they won't let us leave this area of space, but neither do they attempt to kill us.'

'What had happened when we found you then?' asked Susan.

'The same thing that's happened many times before,' said Carol. 'The Sensorites had put us into a deep sleep, which gives the appearance of death . . . And yet they've never tried to destroy us.'

'On the contrary,' continued Maitland, 'we have very hazy memories of them actually returning to our ship from time to time to feed us.'

'But they've never communicated with you?' asked the Doctor.

Maitland shook his head again.

'It just doesn't add up,' said Ian.

'Yes. And that is why you must go at once. Otherwise the Sensorites might try and prevent you from leaving too. You must not delay any longer.'

While Maitland had been speaking Barbara had noticed a faint acrid smell in the air. Now it was stronger. 'I can smell something burning,' she said to Susan.

'Now you mention it, so can I,' the girl agreed.

Neither the Doctor and Ian nor the two astronauts paid the girls much attention. The Doctor, for one, was far more interested in Maitland and Carol's seeming reluctance to talk about the Sensorites. Was there something they were hiding from him?

18

'Surely there must be something we can do for you?' asked Ian.

The Captain shook his head despairingly 'No. No one can help us . . .'

'Couldn't we take them with us in the TARDIS, Grandfather?' asked Susan.

'No. We cannot leave this ship,' said Carol. 'You see, there's . . . there's John to think about . . .'

'John?' The Doctor was immediately intrigued by this new addition to the crew, and by the tremor he detected in Carol's voice when she spoke the name. 'And who might John be, hmm?'

'He's our mineralogist . . .' Carol said. She felt herself suddenly very close to tears.

Barbara interrupted the Doctor's questioning. 'There *is* something burning!' she insisted, her concern growing.

Ian sniffed at the air. 'I think you're right, Barbara. Maitland, you wouldn't have a short circuit, would you?'

'No, that's impossible.'

Barbara moved over to the open door and beckoned Ian to follow her down the corridor. 'It seems to be coming from down here. Let's take a look.'

Relatively unconcerned with what was in all probability an overloaded junction box, the Doctor resumed his conversation with Maitland. He still insisted upon the immediate departure of the TARDIS crew.

'There does seem to be nothing else I can do for you here,' the Doctor admitted, casting a pitying look at Maitland and Carol. There was undoubtedly something they were concealing from him, but he could tell from their determined faces that they would not allow him to help them. Well, if that was their wish, so be it. He made up his mind: 'Goodbye, my friends. Come along, Susan.'

He took his granddaughter's hand and for the second time they sadly took their leave of the flight deck. As they left, Maitland and Carol exchanged looks of relief and regret.

As the Doctor and Susan walked down the corridor which led to the TARDIS they caught up with Ian and Barbara. 'It's stronger down here, Doctor,' Barbara called out from the gloom in which the time-machine had materialised.

'Perhaps it's coming from inside the TARDIS,' the Doctor suggested.

Susan took out her key to open the door. Suddenly she started. 'Grandfather, look!'

The Doctor followed Susan's pointing finger. On the left-hand door of the police telephone box, where there should have been the TARDIS lock, was now nothing but a large hole and a patch of charred woodwork. A few wisps of smoke still hung around the space.

'Good grief!' cried the Doctor indignantly. 'They've taken the lock!'

'No, Grandfather, don't you see?' Susan's voice was now almost hysterical. 'It's not just the lock – it's the whole opening mechanism. The doors are permanently locked!'

'Permanently?' repeated Ian, a hint of panic in his voice. 'There must be a way in,' he insisted. 'Can't we break down the door?'

'And disturb the field dimensions inside the TARDIS?' said the Doctor, outraged at the very idea. 'We dare not! We have been most effectively shut out!'

'The Sensorites?' asked Barbara.

'Who else?'

'But why? What do they want from us?'

'I don't know,' admitted the Doctor. 'And for that matter why have they kept those two astronauts in captivity?'

'Grandfather . . .' began Susan. 'What's that? Can't you feel it too?'

At first she had thought it was her imagination, but even as she spoke her companions could also detect a faint vibration in the floor of the spaceship. It rapidly grew stronger, louder, shaking the floor beneath their feet and the walls all around them; shaking the travellers like dice in a can; shaking the entire world. It seemed that the whole spaceship was about to fall apart.

'What is it? What's happening?' cried Ian, his teeth chattering helplessly together. Barbara held her hands over her mouth, fearful that the stomach-churning vibration would make her vomit.

'Back to the flight deck! Quickly!' commanded the Doctor. As the four time-travellers stumbled back down the corridor, hopelessly attempting to keep their balance in this madness, the frightening reality of their situation crashed down on each of them.

They were marooned, separated from the safety of the TARDIS, alone in the unimaginable emptiness of space.

Totally helpless, they were at the unrelenting mercy of unseen foes who lurked in the shadows. Unseen foes who could invade the inviolable sanctity of the TARDIS. Unseen foes who seemed intent to tear apart this spaceship as a child would an unwanted toy.

Helpless. Alone. *Afraid*.

The Sensorites were in control.

2

War of Nerves

The Doctor's party burst onto the flight deck and onto a scene of barely supressed hysteria. Maitland and Carol were in a state of semi-shock, almost unable to move, and seemingly powerless to operate the ship's controls.

They sat trembling at their consoles, their hands pressed to their temples as though to shut out the mind-jarring vibration all around them. Carol was moaning over and over to herself: 'Get back . . . get away . . .'

The Doctor grabbed Maitland by the shoulders and shook him vigorously. 'What is it, man?' he demanded. 'Can't you control your own ship?'

Maitland looked at the Doctor in despair. 'It . . . it's no use,' he stammered, 'I . . . I'm powerless. The Sensorites are stronger than I am.'

Recognising that Maitland could be of no help to them, the Doctor pushed him aside and took charge in the midst of the chaos. A glance at the control panels told him that the ship was veering wildly off its predetermined course.

'Which is your parallel thrust?' he demanded of the terrified captain. Maitland gestured to a bank of levers to the left of the control panel, and the Doctor immediately initialled a series of delicate adjustments to the orbital balance. Addressing Ian who had joined the whimpering Carol by the navigation console, he snapped, 'Velocity, Chesterton. Check it!'

'It's not registering, Doctor!' he said through clenched teeth.

Maitland looked at the Doctor in wild-eyed terror: 'To try and control the spaceship is suicide, I tell you!'

'Oh, do go away!' The Doctor dismissed him and then reconsidered: 'Which are the stabilisers? Think, man!'

Maitland pointed a quivering finger to the controls. With a preciseness all the more remarkable in the circumstances the

Doctor eased the stabilisers into place.

Almost as quickly as it had begun the shuddering of the ship ceased and relative peace returned once more to the flight deck.

'There!' beamed the Doctor, smug satisfaction filling his face. 'All systems are steady. The ship was spinning about on its axis,' he explained.

But they were far from safe. As soon as one horrifying fate was averted, a new danger threatened. Turning to the observation port, they saw the yellow orb of the Sense-Sphere appearing brighter and larger than before. The spaceship was on a collision course, heading straight for the planet!

'Where are your deflection beams, Maitland?' asked the Doctor.

'There,' he replied, indicating a series of red buttons on a white panel. 'But it's useless, I tell you . . . useless . . .' he repeated.

'Pschaw!' The Doctor made obvious his contempt for Maitland's defeatism. '*I'll* see about that! Velocity reading, please.'

Happy to have something to take her mind off the surrounding chaos, Carol replied, 'Mach three . . . and increasing.'

The Sense-Sphere now filled the entire view port. It was Ian's turn to panic. 'We're only nineteen miles to the nearest point of impact!' he cried.

'Barbara!' cried Susan, automatically clutching her teacher's arm. 'We're going to crash!'

Calm among the pandemonium, the Doctor barked out his orders as he adjusted the ship's controls. 'Check course now!'

'We're lifting slightly,' said Ian. 'But the velocity's still increasing.'

'Check reverse thrust to starboard—now!'

'Doctor!' screamed Carol, 'we're increasing to mach four. We're still going down! We're heading for point of impact!'

The Doctor turned to Maitland. 'Boost the engines,' he ordered. 'Engage forward thrust.'

The captain looked blankly at the old man. He was totally immobile in his terror.

'Oh, for heaven's sake, man!' cried the Doctor. He pushed

past Maitland again and pulled down the main booster lever in front of him.

Instantly the view of the Sense-Sphere dropped from the observation port, as the spaceship responded to the Doctor's adjustments and shot out of its collision course.

In the general sigh of relief, Maitland sat alone, his face covered in a cold sweat. Like a man possessed he looked at the main booster lever which he had failed to engage and then back at his trembling hands.

'Why couldn't I do it?' he asked despairingly. 'Why couldn't I do it?'

A little while later everything had returned to its semblance of normality and the spaceship had resumed its usual orbit of the Sense-Sphere. Barbara and Susan had left the flight deck to prepare a meal from the spacecraft's supply of iron and protein concentrates, while the Doctor assessed the situation to an audience of Ian, Carol and a still shaken Captain Maitland.

'You know,' said the Doctor, 'these Sensorites weren't trying to kill us at all. I think what we've just undergone was an exercise in fear and power. They have incredible mental facilities – we've all experienced how they can control our minds.'

'Yes,' agreed Carol, 'but for some reason your minds aren't as open to them as ours are.'

'And you, my dear, found a way to resist them,' he reminded her. 'Whereas our friend Maitland's power to resist them was taken from him.'

'I was afraid,' Maitland said simply. 'All my training and I was so afraid I couldn't even move.' He was totally, utterly despondent.

Ian laid a reassuring hand on his shoulder. 'No, you weren't,' he said kindly. 'They just made you feel hopeless.'

'Quite right, Chesterton,' the Doctor said. 'You know, it's all quite extraordinary. These Sensorites are dangerous and cunning, certainly, but that's not all. They can control, they can frighten – but they don't attempt to kill. Furthermore, they feed you and keep you alive up here in that death-like trance. Now, why are you so important to them, hmm?'

Maitland and Carol exchanged blank looks. There was no imaginable reason for the Sensorites' apparent desire to keep them prisoner in eternal orbit around the Sense-Sphere. If they posed a threat to the aliens surely it would be better to kill them, rather than take all this trouble to keep them alive and healthy? And why had they so efficiently marooned the Doctor and his friends? Did the Sensorites have some terrible unknown plans for them?

'Has either of you ever seen or met these creatures?' asked the Doctor.

Carol nodded sadly. 'John has . . .'

'Ah yes, your mineralogist,' said the Doctor. 'I'd like to have a talk with him.'

'I'm afraid that's quite out of the question,' snapped Maitland, suddenly on the defensive.

The Doctor raised an enquiring eyebrow. 'Really? And why not?' he asked, aware of the raw nerve he had touched in both Maitland and Carol.

Maitland dismissed the Doctor's insistent questioning with a shrug of the shoulders. 'I – I don't want to talk about it . . .' he said lamely.

The Doctor looked curiously at the two astronauts who avoided his gaze. A sixth sense was buzzing in his mind. At last he had found the key which might begin to unlock this mystery.

That key was John.

Barbara and Susan stood alone in the gloom of a small passageway, unsure of which way to turn. They had come to a dead end and were faced with a choice of two doors to take. Barbara secretly suspected that they had taken a wrong turning, but said nothing to Susan. To be lost in this maze of half-lit corridors was not something to be desired: it was hardly worth alarming Susan.

She indicated the right-hand door. 'Let's try this one. I'm sure Carol said that the ship's galley was this way – though I really can't imagine a kitchen on board a ship like this . . .'

'Oh, it won't be anything like you've seen,' Susan said cheerily. 'Just stocks of iron and protein pills – and recycled water,' she added mischievously.

Barbara made a face of mock horror and disgust, and pressed her hand on the touch-sensitive panel by the door. The large circular door opened, sliding soundlessly upwards.

As she and Susan passed through the doorway they failed to notice a dark form detach itself from the shadows at the far end of the room. Slowly, relentlessly, it shuffled after them.

'Hey, this is brilliant!' Susan exclaimed upon entering the room. 'It's a library!' She indicated the rows of shelves containing microfilm and log books, and the study desks, each with its own microfiche reader.

'I don't think we should stay here,' Barbara advised. 'Let's get back to the others.' She was now certain that they had indeed lost their way, and in the dimmed lighting of the ship's interior that odd sense of unease she had felt before was returning.

There was something not quite right here. The rhythmic pulse of the life support system sounded strange, as if another noise had been added to it, a harsh, irregular sound, almost like . . .

She nearly jumped out of her skin when Susan clicked on the microreader. The harsh light from it threw three grotesque moving shadows on the wall.

Three.

Susan was absorbed in reading the microfiche entries. 'Barbara, look at this – it's a log of the ships's journey. The last entry seems to have been made over a year ago. They dropped most of the crew off at Space Station Two-Alpha-Five and were on their way home when –' The grim realisation suddenly struck her: 'Barbara, they've been asleep for *thirteen months!*'

But Barbara was in no mood to listen as she silently drew Susan's attention to the doorway and the lumbering shape which stood before them.

Silhouetted against the light it stood motionless, challenging Barbara and Susan. As it staggered slowly towards the two terrified girls the light from the microreader cast a macabre light on its face, revealing a shock of white hair and two unblinking white eyes staring out from a deeply lined and careworn face.

Susan clutched Barbara in terror: 'What is it, Barbara?

27

Back on the flight deck the Doctor and Ian continued their relentless questioning of Maitland and Carol about the third member of their crew.

'Don't you see?' argued Ian, infuriated at the astronauts' apparent unwillingness to understand. 'John might be able to give us some valuable information about the Sensorites.'

'I told you – you can't see him.' Carol's steely defiance was matched by Maitland who answered the Doctor and Ian's questions with an impassive, emotionless stare.

The situation was hopeless, thought Ian. Maitland and Carol were locked in a conspiracy of silence. In an attempt to break the tension he asked casually, 'What's keeping Barbara and Susan? I'm starving.'

That seemingly careless remark suddenly galvanised the two astronauts into action. Maitland sped over to the main exit door through which Barbara and Susan had gone in search of the ship's galley. Hoping against all odds, he waved his hand over the opening mechanism.

Locked.

He turned despairingly to Carol. 'We should have warned them!'

'The door must have been locked from the other side,' she said and then addressed the Doctor and Ian: 'Quickly – they're in danger. We must get in from the other door.' She ushered Maitland and the bewildered time-travellers to a secondary exit door at the far end of the flight deck. That too was now locked.

The Doctor grabbed Maitland. 'What is it, man? What is going on behind that door?' he demanded, his concern for Susan's safety evident in his voice.

'It's no use,' Maitland said, all hope gone. 'There's nothing we can do for them. We can't get off the flight deck . . .'

'Who's done this?' asked Ian, pointing at the two locked doors. A dreadful fear crept over him as he asked, 'Are there Sensorites in there?'

It was a man, gaunt and emaciated, looking more dead than alive, but a man nevertheless. His wide, maniacally staring eyes bulged out of their sockets as he stumbled remorselessly towards Barbara and Susan.

The girls were cowering in a darkened corner of the library, scared out of their wits. As he drew nearer to them he held out his arms, almost in a gesture of supplication. Suddenly he stumbled and fell to his knees at the girls' feet.

Seizing this opportunity, Barbara and Susan took flight, rushing past the man, out of the library and into the passage outside. But to their horror the exit from the passage had now been locked. As they struggled to pull open the door, which opened outwards, they were aware of the crazed man following them once more, his breathing harsher this time, and his footsteps sounding somehow even more menacing . . .

He was within almost a foot of them when he suddenly pressed his hands to his throbbing temples and let a cry of anguish escape from his dried and cracked lips. And then, to Barbara and Susan's utter astonishment, he turned around and rushed wailing down the corridor.

While the Doctor and Ian were busy attempting to override the locking mechanism of the flight deck's main exit door, Maitland and Carol were standing some way back, engaged in a fierce but whispered argument.

'We've been over this a hundred times before, Carol,' Maitland hissed. 'We must not go after John.'

'But the other times the Sensorites made the decision for us,' countered Carol. 'The Doctor and the others have shown us that we *can* resist them. It's only fear that makes us weak.'

'Carol, it's too dangerous,' Maitland pleaded. He remembered all too well his own fear when the Sensorites took control of the ship.

'What you mean is, *I* mustn't go in there,' accused Carol 'You're afraid for me . . .'

Maitland's voice was suddenly tender and sympathetic. 'I know how much John meant to you, Carol.'

Carol sighed, pained by the memory. 'The last time I saw him he didn't even know my name . . . But I must see him and find out. Besides, there's Barbara and Susan to think about.'

'Maitland!' called Ian, angered at his and Carol's lack of

assistance. 'Help us get through this door!'

Finally swayed not by Ian's anger but by Carol's sad determination Maitland shook himself into action. 'Yes . . . we have some cutting equipment here – I'll get it rigged up and cut through this lock.'

'Well, get on with it then!'

His attempt to open the door finally having met with failure, Ian walked over to Carol. 'Tell me,' he said, 'what *is* it you're afraid of?'

Carol turned away, not wanting Ian to see the tears which were welling up in her eyes. 'John is in there,' she said. 'He and I were going to get married when we got back to the Earth. But we arrived here and . . . and the Sensorites affected him far more than Captain Maitland and myself. I . . . I had to sit here helplessly and watch him get worse and worse . . . It was terrible . . .'

'So they've taken over his mind,' Ian said gently. 'What's it done to him?'

'He'll be frightened of strangers. He may become violent . . .'

Barbara and Susan cautiously ventured down the passageway, looking warily around for any sign of their pursuer. But he seemed to have vanished, disappeared once more into the dark shadows which had so effectively concealed him.

Suddenly the lights were switched on, temporarily blinding the girls whose eyes were unaccustomed to such cutting brilliance on board this gloomy spaceship. They steeled themselves for an attack.

It was an attack which never came. Before them, now fully visible in the harsh glare, was the madman, who once again fell down at Barbara's feet and emitted a long sorrowful moan.

Susan looked down at him in disbelief. 'He's *crying*,' she said.

'Who – who are you?' the man asked, his tear-stained face looking up into Barbara's eyes. 'You're like my sisters . . . Have you come to help me?' His voice was plaintive, like a little lost child's.

Barbara bent down on one knee and held the man's hand in

hers. In the light and close up he didn't look so terrifying after all, she thought; in fact, he looked more like a frightened little boy.

'Are you one of the crew of the spaceship?' she asked, noticing for the first time his grey uniform. 'Do you want us to help you?'

The man nodded frantically, tears of delight and relief streaming down his face. 'John,' he said. 'My name is John.'

'Don't be afraid, John, we'll take care of you,' Barbara promised him, cradling his sobbing head in her arms. She suddenly looked for all the world like a teacher, comforting nothing more than a bullied child at Coal Hill School.

'Can't you work any faster?' demanded the Doctor, irritated and impatient. 'My granddaughter's in there!'

Maitland had opened up a storage locker and taken out a small cutting tool, in appearance much like a pencil torch. He was now applying its thin laser beam around the locking mechanism of the main door. But the process was painfully slow. As the Doctor and Ian stood by helplessly they had more than enough time to think of the terrible things which might be happening to Barbara and Susan on the other side of the door.

'We should be through the lock very shortly,' Maitland told them from his crouched position by the door. Suddenly he stopped and looked up. His eyes met Carol's and a glimmer of fear and recognition passed between them.

'What is it now!' cried the Doctor, totally at odds with Maitland. 'Do get on with it!'

Maitland waved for the Doctor to be silent. 'Listen,' he whispered. 'Can't you hear it?'

Impressed by the urgency in his voice the Doctor and Ian stood to attention. Yes, there was something: a quiet hiss at first but now growing louder and louder into a high-pitched whine, like finger nails being drawn repeatedly across a blackboard. It came from the sub-space audio receivers by the command console.

Carol was the first to speak and there was no mistaking the nervous apprehension in her voice. 'It's the Sensorites,' she said. 'That interference is caused by the machines which

31

carry them through space . . .'

Fighting the fear already mounting within him, Maitland abruptly took charge of the situation. 'Carol, get back to your instruments,' he ordered. 'Doctor, will you take the controller's seat?'

As the Doctor hurriedly complied, Ian moved over to the observation window. Moving rapidly towards the spaceship were two tiny pin-pricks of light.

'Are those the Sensorites?' he asked. Maitland nodded. 'But they must be miles away,' Ian continued.

'It won't take them long to get here,' remarked the captain wryly. 'The Sensorite travel-machines move at unbelievable speeds.'

Ian turned to the Doctor for confirmation. The old man nodded. 'Remember, Chesterton, they've been here once already. They took the TARDIS lock.'

'You mean, you think they took it back down to their planet?'

'Yes. And now they're coming back. With what orders, I wonder? To take over our minds? Or to kill us?'

'We're not going to be destroyed,' Maitland said wearily. 'If they intended that they could have done it many times before.'

'If that collision course was their idea of a joke I'd hate to be one of their enemies,' Ian added bitterly.

Carol turned to him from her position at the navigation console. 'They weren't really trying to crash us, Ian. They just keep on playing this horrible game of nerves, breaking our will to resist . . .'

'But there must be something we can do!' he insisted. 'We can't just sit around and wait for them to arrive!'

'*That's all we can do!*' Carol retorted.

'But surely we can take steps to protect ourselves?'

The Doctor joined in the argument. 'My dear Chesterton, it's our minds they take over. So we have to assume that the brain is all-important. Now, let our intelligence be our own defence – and attack!'

Ian was about to counter with his own arguments, but stopped dead. The high-pitched whine from the Sensorites' travel-machines which had reached an almost unbearable crescendo had stopped. The flight deck was plunged into a sudden eerie silence.

Ian looked at his three companions. Maitland and Carol were staring past him, looking with stunned recognition at the observation port behind him. Even the Doctor's face betrayed an unaccustomed and uncomfortable expression of fear.

Slowly Ian turned around to see what the others were staring at in the port.

White and ghost-like against the blackness of space a figure floated by the spaceship. The creature's lack of any apparent spacesuit or breathing apparatus made it seem almost supernaturally impervious to the sub-zero temperature outside, or the lack of air. The long elegant fingers of its outstretched hands guided it slowly along the outside hull of the ship, while its bulbous head searched this way and that for entry.

Sensing the humans on the flight deck it tilted its head towards them, allowing them to look into an alien face which returned their gaze with cold, unblinking eyes. It regarded them curiously, observing them as one would specimens in a zoo. As the creature continued its steady appraising stare, the Doctor, Ian, Maitland and Carol all felt a thrill of spine-chilling terror.

The Sensorites had arrived.

The Dreams of Avarice

The Doctor glared at the alien being in the observation port with arrogant defiance, as though he were engaged in a massive battle of wills. Without taking his eyes off the creature he reached out for Ian's trembling arm.

'Steady, Chesterton,' he said. 'The calmer you are, the stronger you will be.'

Ian indicated Maitland who sat transfixed by his console. He waved a hand in front of his face, but the captain's unblinking eyes did not register the schoolteacher's presence: all they seemed to see was the alien at the window, gazing in at them.

The Doctor nodded his head: 'Fear, my boy – that's what it is. It's loosened his mind: it gives the Sensorites the power to control it.'

Turning away from the alien in the observation port, he went over to the captain and fixed him with an almost hypnotic stare. 'Maitland, can you hear me?' he said. 'There's work to be done. I need you!'

Such was the power in the Doctor's call to his sense of duty that Maitland began to stir. The Doctor continued his appeal: 'There's a door to be opened! Remember? Danger on the other side!'

Suddenly aware of his obligations to those on board his ship, Maitland snapped out of his trance-like state. 'Yes, of course,' he said. 'We must save the girls!'

As Maitland applied himself once more to the task of breaking through the locked door, the Doctor turned back to the observation port and smiled smugly to himself. His suspicions had been confirmed: now that the fear had been broken, the Sensorite was nowhere to be seen.

Feeling ineffectual beside Maitland, with nothing to do but stand and wait, Ian was quickly becoming impatient with the captain's slow progress. It seemed to be taking forever for him to make even the slightest impression on the lock, during which time any manner of thing could be happening to Barbara and Susan.

He voiced his fears to the Doctor who wagged an admonishing finger at him. 'Don't you think I'm not concerned too, Chesterton?' he asked. 'But we must contain our emotions. Otherwise, they confuse the brain and leave it wide open to the Sensorites. Look at poor Maitland: fear and inertia have left him vulnerable.'

Carol who had been trying unsuccessfully to override the locking mechanism of the door from the control panels, suddenly stood stock-still. So abrupt was her action that the other three turned to look at her. She pointed to a diagrammatic map of the ship displayed on a screen before her; a green light was blinking in one section of the plan.

'The Sensorites have come aboard,' she explained slowly.

'*What!*' bellowed Ian. Was nothing secure on this ship of incompetents? 'How the hell did they get in?'

'Through the loading bay,' Carol said. 'They have some way of overriding our security systems . . .'

'Then Barbara and Susan are in even greater danger!' cried Ian, a note of hysteria creeping into his voice. He turned back to Maitland. 'For God's sake, man, can't you work any faster?'

'I'm working as fast as I can!' he snapped back. 'It's a very slow process!'

The Doctor hurried over to the two men in an attempt to quell the enmity developing between them. Fear and panic were beginning to take hold of them again: fear for themselves; fear for Barbara and Susan; fear of whatever lay behind the locked door. If they allowed that fear to gain the upper hand the Sensorites would have won.

Ian began to pound uselessly on the door, calling out Barbara and Susan's names.

Barbara looked imploringly into John's tear-stained face. 'All we want you to do is open the door,' she pleaded.

'No!' John was adamant. '*I'll* protect you.'

This is madness, thought Barbara. It was as if John, having at last found someone he could trust, stubbornly wanted to

36

keep them with him forever. Or was that all there was to it . . . ?

Susan continued the argument: 'But please, John: our friends are out there.'

'No – no, they're not. They're dead – all dead,' the deranged astronaut claimed, like a sulky child telling the most terrible lies to keep his new-found friends with him.

'But we were with them just a while ago,' Barbara insisted, and then stopped as John doubled up in pain and fell to the floor, his hands clutching at his temples.

She was instantly at his side. 'What is it, John?' she asked.

But John did not hear her. Instead he looked up, past her and Susan, a glazed look of terror in his eyes. 'Frighten them?' he asked some invisible presence. 'No, I can't do that. Nononono . . .' he sobbed.

Barbara tried to comfort him and cast a questioning look at Susan, who was kneeling down beside them. 'Somebody's talking to him – inside his head,' she explained.

John continued his tortured conversation with the unheard voice: 'No, don't force me . . . I *won't* do it . . .' His knuckles turned white as he pressed ever harder at his head, trying to shut out the dreaded insistent voice which had haunted him for so long. As he did so, Barbara held him tightly in her arms, mentally willing him to win his struggle.

Slowly his sobbing subsided and he looked up into Barbara's eyes. '*They* wanted me to frighten you – but I wouldn't,' he boasted. '*I* didn't give way.'

Barbara stroked his hand gratefully. 'We're not afraid, John,' she told him, 'not now that we have you to protect us.'

'Barbara's right,' Susan reassured him. 'We'll look after each other. That's what friends are for.'

'Friends?' asked John, and Barbara and Susan nodded. 'Friends . . .' he repeated the word so contentedly that Susan half-expected him to put his thumb in his mouth and suck it. Then he sat bolt upright and shouted out an oath of defiance to his unseen assailants. 'No! *They are my friends!*'

Not far from the cabin in which Barbara, Susan and John huddled, a pair of alien figures walked slowly and purposefully through the ship's interconnecting passageways.

Occasionally they stopped and looked around, as if trying to sense the location of the two girls and their tormented charge. After a brief pause they would resume their steady pace.

So synchronised were their silent footsteps that one would have been forgiven for thinking, in the half-light, that they were robots rather than creatures of flesh and blood. They moved remorselessly down the corridors, their eyes fixed straight ahead, apparently unaware of anything but their quarry.

Throughout their progress they did not exchange one single word with each other.

'Barbara, I've got an idea.'

Barbara looked enquiringly at her former pupil who had been pacing about the cabin for some time, increasingly disturbed by the power which the Sensorites seemed able to exercise over John's mind.

'John's quiet now,' she said, 'but we can't be sure that the Sensorites won't make him help them – and attack us. Look, if they can use their brains, why can't we use ours?'

'To defend John, you mean?' Barbara asked, looking down pityingly at him. He was crouched in a corner of the room, rocking to and fro with his hands clasped firmly around his knees.

'*And* ourselves,' Susan stressed. 'Grandfather and I were once on a planet called Esto. The plants there used thought transference to communicate amongst themselves. If you stood in between two of them they sent up a sort of screeching noise. Grandfather said it was because they were aware of another intelligent mind.'

'Breaking in on their conversation?' asked Barbara. 'And blocking it?'

'Exactly!' I thought that if we both tried together, our combined thoughts might be enough to –'

'The Sensorites!' cried John, his face suddenly tense again and his eyes wild with terror. 'They're near us now!'

'This is our chance!' urged Susan. 'We must both think of the same thing at the same time.'

'Think what?' asked Barbara. ' "We defy you." Something like that?'

'Yes! We must concentrate very hard. Ready?'

Barbara nodded: 'All right then: when I count to five. One . . .'

(In the passageway outside the Sensorites stopped, and nodded at each other in silent agreement . . .)

'. . . Two . . .'

(One of the aliens took from a side pouch a strange multi-wired device. It looked rather like a small tennis racquet and seemed to be made out of ivory. He held it up at arm's length and pointed it at the locked door leading to the cabin . . .)

'. . . Three . . .'

(The device began to hum slightly, as it emitted a beam of invisible energy . . .)

'. . . Four . . .'

(Slowly the cabin door began to open . . .)

'. . . Five. Now, Susan, now!'

We defy you. We defy you. We defy you!

(In the passageway the two Sensorites crumpled to the floor, unable to withstand Barbara and Susan's combined act of mental resistance. They writhed in agony, holding their heads as though they were about to burst. Like fish out of water their limbs jerked this way and that as they lost all control over their environment.)

We defy you. We defy you. We defy you!

Exhausted with her mental struggle Susan fainted into Barbara's arms, who lowered her to the ground. After a few minutes Barbara turned around to see the door of the cabin open wide – to reveal an anxious Ian and Maitland who had broken through the main door and had at last found their companions.

The tension finally broken, Barbara rushed sobbing into Ian's arms.

Some time later and reunited with the Doctor and Carol, Barbara and Susan were recovering in the crew lounge just off the flight deck. Maitland and Ian had taken John to his former quarters where he was now sleeping peacefully. When the two men returned to the flight deck it was to a council of war.

The Doctor was looking thoughtfully at his granddaughter who was stretched out on a sofa sipping at a drink of protein concentrate.

'It might be possible for Susan's thoughts to reach out to the Sensorites,' he surmised.

'So we really can resist and fight them?' asked Carol.

'*And* communicate with them!' added the Doctor pertinently.

'I heard hundreds of voices in my head, Grandfather,' Susan said, gently massaging her forehead.

'And that was a very dangerous thing to do,' chided the old man. 'Because you were strong-willed and without fear they couldn't harm you. Whereas our friend John . . . How is he?' he asked as Ian and Maitland walked onto the flight deck.

'He's resting now, but he looks so old,' answered Maitland. 'Did you know his hair was almost completely white?'

The Doctor raised himself to his full height and glared down at Maitland with a look usually reserved for fools and pompous officials. 'There's nothing wrong with that,' he declared, stroking his own silver mane.

'In a man of thirty, Doctor?' Maitland threw up his hands in despair. 'What have the Sensorites done to him? What do they want from us?'

'Doctor,' began Ian, 'John muttered something to me just before he passed out: it sounded like "the dreams of avarice".' The Doctor shrugged his shoulders, unable to guess the significance of the remark, and urged Ian to continue. 'On Earth we have a saying: "rich beyond the dreams of avarice" . . .' Ian warmed to his theme. 'John was the ship's mineralogist, wasn't he? I think he discovered something the Sensorites wanted kept secret. That's why he's had the worst of it: the Sensorites silenced him and kept Carol and Maitland prisoners above their planet.'

'I see . . . and now they're trying to do the same to us by taking the lock of the TARDIS . . .' The Doctor studied Ian with reluctant admiration, and rubbed his hands with glee. 'Chesterton, my boy, I do believe you've hit on the answer!'

Not far away in another part of the ship, the two Sensorites had now recovered from their mental attack. They talked to

40

each other in hushed voices. One of them held a white disc to his forehead.

'I have communicated with the First Elder,' he said. 'He says he is interested in the human voice which said "we defy you".'

'These Earth-creatures which are newly arrived seem to possess more intelligence than the others. We cannot control their minds as easily . . .'

His companion hesitated a moment, using the ivory disc to communicate with his home planet thousands of miles away. Then he continued: 'It is because they have less fear of us. We are to stay here and watch and listen to them closely. If they try to attack us with force we are to summon our Warriors – and destroy them.'

On the flight deck the time-travellers and Maitland and Carol were gathered around a spectrograph which was located in a small alcove near the navigation console. It was here, Carol explained, that John was first attacked by the Sensorites while he was making a routine survey of the Sense-Sphere.

With his glasses perched on his beak-like nose, the Doctor studied the read-outs from the spectrograph: long strips of light sensitive paper patterned with vertical bands of colour. By examining the colour and width of the bands, which were caused by the radioactive emissions of certain minerals, it was possible to determine the exact geological composition of any planet. Unable to spot anything out of the ordinary, he passed the print-out over to Ian who looked at it closely before reaching the same conclusion: the Sense-Sphere was a perfectly ordinary planet, circling a perfectly ordinary star. He handed the results back to the Doctor.

'It's no use,' Maitland told them. 'I studied the readings whenever I could, but there didn't seem to be anything which could be of any importance. The Sense-Sphere is a completely average planet with a slightly larger land mass than usual – but that's all.'

'Yes, yes, I suppose you're right. You know I was so sure . . .' sighed the Doctor, thoughtfully rubbing his chin. Finally he admitted defeat and tossed the graph onto an adjacent work table. As it fell his eyes caught the bands of colour at a different angle. He immediately snatched the read-out back and excitedly showed it to the others.

'Look! I knew it was there all the time! But it's all diffused and mixed up with the other elements!' He pointed enthusiastically at several thin bands on the graph: 'There –and there – and there!'

'But what is it, Doctor?' asked Ian.

'Molybdenum!'

Barbara looked blankly at the old man and pressed for a further explanation.

'It's used as an alloy in steel,' Maitland said. 'It's able to withstand extremely high temperatures. It's a major part of all our spacecraft: most of the galaxy's space fleets would be useless without it.'

'Precisely!' exclaimed the Doctor. 'Iron melts at 1539 degrees Centigrade—but molybdenum melts at 2622 degrees Centigrade. It's the perfect alloy for travel in hyper space. In terms of usage it's one of the most precious minerals in the galaxy. No wonder John was excited: that planet down there must be full of it. It's a veritable gold mine!'

('They know too much.' 'Agreed. We must strike now.')

The attacks which they had experienced before were nothing compared to what hit Maitland and Carol as the Doctor spoke those words, and in so doing finally revealed the secret of the Sensorites.

The strength of this offence was almost tangible: the astronauts collapsed onto the floor, their faces wracked with unbearable pain and horror. The Doctor and Susan bent over their jerking bodies, powerless to protect the astronauts from a force which seemed to be almost physical rather than mental.

Carol screamed out in agony as the Sensorites took possession of the fear already within her mind and magnified it a thousand fold; Maitland flailed about like a helpless child, scared half to death.

Ian looked down grimly at the two pitiful victims of the Sensorites' power. He was sick and tired of just sitting around, doing nothing, waiting for the Sensorites to take over their minds one by one. Leaving the Doctor and Susan to offer what comfort they could to the astronauts, he grabbed

Barbara's arm and headed for the exit: 'Come on, Barbara. Let's find them.'

It was time to face their fear.

The most basic fear of all is the fear of the unknown, and as Ian and Barbara walked down the dim passageways and half-lit corridors of the ship, past the all-enveloping inky black shadows, they relived all their childhood fears. Once again they were little children, climbing the stairs in the dark, not knowing what manner of unearthly horror awaited them at the top.

The slightest sound they heard was amplified, perverted and transformed into the malevolent hissing of a goblin, or the mocking laughter of a devil. Behind every half-opened door an evil spirit was lurking, and the bogey-man made ready to leap out at them from any darkened corner.

But these evil spirits and bogey-men were hideously – cruelly – real, and as they made their slow and careful way they were grateful for the other's hand in theirs.

Ian paused by a closed door and listened. Nothing. Cautiously he pushed it open and peered through into an adjoining room. It seemed to be some sort of rest area. Motioning Barbara to follow, he led the way through the room until they came to a door at the far end.

It was slightly ajar.

'Where do you suppose this leads?' whispered Barbara.

'Let's find out.' Ian noticed Barbara's trembling lips. 'You needn't come if you don't want to,' he said.

'Nonsense,' she replied, smiling for his benefit. She knew that Ian was just as terrified as she was, but there was no going back for either of them. Whatever lay in that terrible space beyond the door had to be faced; and they needed each other now as never before.

The door swung open easily and the teachers passed into the room beyond.

It seemed to be a storage area, piled high with crates and boxes, and lined with aisles of shelves containing discarded equipment: perfect cover for hidden enemies.

Suddenly Ian felt Barbara's free hand grab his arm, her nails almost digging into his flesh. She nodded over to the far corner of the room.

There, standing just out of the shadows, waiting patiently for Ian and Barbara, were two unearthly creatures.

They had found the Sensorites.

4

The Unwilling Warriors

In appearance the Sensorites were exactly the same. To Ian and Barbara they seemed no less than a set of ghastly twins.

Their bone-white heads were bulbous, with an enlarged cranium tapering down to a small v-shaped chin covered with wisps of snow-white whiskers. These rose on either side of their jaws to end just above their tiny cat-like ears which were covered with a fibrous membrane. Along their temples were two ice-blue veins which pulsed rhythmically as the Sensorites regarded the humans before them with an almost Oriental inscrutability.

Their eyes were their most disquieting feature. Small, dark and lidless, they betrayed no emotion whatsoever, making it impossible for Ian and Barbara to know their thoughts or intentions. They were surmounted on prominent cheekbones which, together with their whiskers, gave the Sensorites an aged, wizened appearance.

A bony protruberance in the middle of their faces was the only evidence of a nose which evolution had deemed no longer necessary for their survival. Beneath their beards a small mouth twitched, but made no sound.

Little more than five feet high, they were each dressed in a one-piece, high-necked grey tunic, across the arms of which were three broad black bands. Hanging by plastic strips from each of their belts was a white disc: one Sensorite also carried a small racquet-like device which seemed to be made of some kind of ivory.

The most bizarre thing about them was their feet which were flat, circular pads about eighteen inches in diameter. Despite their clumsy appearance they enabled the Sensorites to move with an almost feline grace, making not a sound on the metal floor of the storeroom. As they advanced upon Ian and Barbara they moved in perfect unison, each one knowing exactly what the other one was thinking.

Like helpless mice face-to-face with a cat, Ian and Barbara stood transfixed to the spot by the Sensorites' glare and the waves of fear which emanated from them.

They struggled painfully against their emotions, tried to rationalise their terror. Slowly they began to back away from the Sensorites who continued their relentless advance.

As the two humans retreated down the aisles of the store-room, never once taking their eyes off the approaching aliens, Ian grabbed a large iron spanner from one of the equipment shelves. He raised it threateningly at the Sensorites who instinctively cowered away.

The two groups stood motionless, glaring at each other, daring the other to make the next move. After what seemed like an eternity the Sensorites resumed their steady pace towards the two terror-struck teachers.

At last Ian and Barbara reached the half-open door; they passed through it and slammed it shut with a gasp of relief.

'Find Maitland,' ordered Ian. 'Ask him how to lock these doors. We must keep the Sensorites confined to this area of the ship.'

Barbara began to protest but Ian cut her short: 'Don't worry about me! Go!'

She nodded meekly and rushed off as the door leading to the storeroom opened, allowing the Sensorites to pass through. Ian moved back again, his body tensed, and the knuckles of his hand showing white as he grasped the spanner tightly.

'Who are you?' he demanded of the aliens. 'What do you want?'

No reply.

'Goddam it, why won't you speak?'

As if in reply, one of the Sensorites raised its arm and extended a long-fingered hand towards Ian's forehead.

He jumped away instantly, once more raising the spanner above his head, ready to strike. Again the Sensorites reacted to his threat of physical violence by taking a step backwards, before resuming their silent, terrifying approach.

Back on the flight deck Maitland and Carol had recovered physically from the Sensorites' attack; mentally, however,

46

they were still in a state of acute shock. Barbara was desperately trying to wrench from Maitland instructions as to how to confine the Sensorites to that part of the ship where they now were.

'It's no use, Barbara,' the Doctor said, turning away from Carol's impassive form. 'This poor girl's just the same. They'll recover shortly but now – when we need them the most – they're useless. Try the sick member of the crew.'

'But he'll be in no position to help,' protested Barbara.

'Just do as I say!'

It seemed almost inhumanly cruel to wake John up from the first untroubled sleep he had had for months . . . but it was the only chance they had left. Barbara hurried out of the flight deck and down the short way to John's cabin.

She roused him from his sleep, begging with him to help them against the creatures he feared most in this world. Wouldn't he try and do it – for his friends? He nodded bravely and allowed Barbara to escort him to the storeroom.

As Barbara helped him along the passageway in search of Ian and the Sensorites they formed a pitiful spectacle: a half-deranged astronaut and a schoolteacher centuries out of her time, and both scared nearly to death.

When they finally found Ian in a secondary corridor he was still engaged in his macabre dance with the aliens, raising his spanner menacingly at them as he backed out through yet another door. Taking his eyes off the aliens for the first time, he turned with glad relief to his two friends. Barbara urged John to lock the door. She looked on with an almost maternal pride as John challenged the Sensorites.

He regarded them nervously for a few seconds and then slammed the door shut in their faces. He keyed out a combination on a small multi-squared panel at the side of the door. Smiling with pleasure he turned to Barbara. 'They can't open it now—*I* made sure of that.'

Without really thinking what she was doing Barbara hugged him: it was the only way there was of expressing thanks to a child who had just faced his greatest fear for the sake of his friends.

Then she turned to Ian with concern. 'Are you all right?' she asked. 'They didn't harm you?'

'No . . .' Ian said thoughtfully. 'I think they were as frightened of me as I was of them . . .'

'Yes, they're not very aggressive, are they . . .' Barbara said, begining to wonder if things were quite as simple as they appeared to be. 'Come on, let's get back to the others.'

When they reached the flight deck they found the Doctor and Susan fussing over Maitland and Carol who had started emerging from their state of shock. They looked up in surprise as Ian's party burst through the open door. Barbara instructed John to lock that door too.

As the door slid slowly down into place, Ian turned to the Doctor and Susan, his face set in defiance. 'Now we'll see what these Sensorites can do.'

Even the advanced technology of the twenty-eighth century was no match for the science of the Sensorites. Using the small racquet-like device it was a relatively simple matter for them to burn through the locking mechanism of the door which John had closed on them.

They walked without haste down the passage leading to the flight deck. When they reached the large circular door, the armed Sensorite raised his device again, but his companion stayed his arm and shook his head. There was a better way . . .

A flash of unspoken agreement passed between them, and they both raised the ivory discs which they carried at their sides to their foreheads. The veins at their temples pulsed even more strongly as they used the discs to reach out to the one person on board the ship who would hear and understand them.

While the others were busy discussing means of fighting back at the Sensorites, and indeed what plans the Sensorites might have for them, Susan had distanced herself from her companions. She could feel a tingling at the back of her skull and seemed to hear a voice – or rather a whisper – echo somewhere inside her mind. The voice seemed to be coming from a very long way away.

As she concentrated, the sound of her friends' conversation grew fainter as the 'inner' voice resolved itself into something much more distinct.

'Yes. But they won't agree to that!' she said suddenly.

The others looked up in astonishment at Susan's outburst. 'Agree?' asked the Doctor. 'What on Earth are you talking about, child?'

'I'm sure they'll talk to you,' Susan continued, not hearing her grandfather's question. Then she turned and addressed her bewildered companions. 'The Sensorites want to know if it's all right for them to talk to you,' she explained.

'You mean to say you've actually made mental contact with them?' asked an incredulous Ian. Was there no end to his former pupil's strange talents?

'Of course we shall see them,' announced the Doctor. 'But they must agree not to harm us. Otherwise I shall fight them,' he warned.

Susan nodded and turned away again. She pressed her hands to her temples and stared blankly into space as she tried once more to make telepathic contact with the Sensorites. Unskilled at telepathy, she silently mouthed her words as she communicated them to the aliens.

After a short while she walked, as if in a dream, to the main exit door and unlocked it, following John's previous actions in reverse. The door slid smoothly upwards to reveal the two figures of the waiting Sensorites. They stepped cautiously onto the flight deck.

Their effect upon the humans was immediate. Maitland and Carol cowered away from the creatures they had lived in fear of for so long; John who had been sitting slouched in a corner began to whimper to himself; Ian and Barbara, seeing their pursuers for the first time in the full light rather than the shadows of the rest of the ship, watched with apprehension as they surveyed the flight deck.

The Doctor regarded them with the same searching curiosity he accorded all new life forms. Only Susan was unmoved, standing by the door in her half-trance state.

'Which one is the Doctor?' one Sensorite asked the other.

'The one with the long white hair.'

The Sensorites' voices were husky and soft, almost a whisper; a fact the Doctor did not hesitate to point out. He hated not being able to listen on to a conversation, especially when it was so obviously about him.

'Speak up,' he demanded imperiously. 'I can't hear you.'

'We apologise,' said the first Sensorite, raising his voice slightly. 'We were talking to each other.'

'What is it you want of us?' the Doctor asked sharply. 'Why don't you let these Earth people go home, hmm?'

The first Sensorite moved further into the room; only the Doctor did not back away from him.

'None of you can ever again leave the area of the Sense-Sphere.' The statement was final and unequivocal.

'Why not?' asked Ian.

'You know the answer to that . . .'

'Molybdenum,' he said, and saw the Sensorite bow his head in confirmation. 'But we're not interested in it.'

'So you say,' said the second Sensorite. 'Once before we trusted Earthmen – to our great cost. They came to the Sense-Sphere and caused us a terrible affliction. We shall not allow it to happen again.'

'What do you expect us to do?' asked Maitland, over-coming his innate fear of the aliens. 'Drift around in space forever?'

'No,' answered the second Sensorite. 'Your case has been debated and it has been decided that you must all come back with us. A special area has been prepared on the Sense-Sphere where you will live and be looked after.'

'These people cannot possibly agree to your demands,' retorted the Doctor.

'We do not wish to harm you, but you will do exactly as we tell you. You have no choice.' The first Sensorite's voice was flat and emotionless.

'But my party *does* have a choice,' the Doctor claimed. 'I assure you we have no intention of spending the rest of our lives with you. You must get off this ship!'

'What will happen if we refuse?'

'Then we will attack you,' joined in Ian.

The second Sensorite pointed to Maitland, Carol and John who were watching the scene, frozen in fear. 'The other Earth people will not be able to help you,' he stated simply.

'Surely we've proved that we don't need any help,' said Barbara.

The Sensorite's response was quick and frighteningly true: 'You have only proved that you can lock doors. We can unlock them.'

'Talking of locks,' said the Doctor indignantly, 'you took the lock from my ship – I want it back immediately!'

'You are in no position to threaten us,' the first Sensorite reminded him. There was a small touch of arrogance in his voice.

Determined to teach these impertinent creatures a lesson they would not forget, the Doctor said, 'I don't make idle threats – but I do keep promises. And I promise you that I can cause you more trouble than you ever dreamed possible if you do not return my property!'

It was no mean boast, as many people from the Doctor's past could testify; but its effect upon the Sensorites was extraordinary – and totally unexpected. As the Doctor raised his voice in anger and outrage, the Sensorites staggered away from him, clutching their ears in pain. It was as though the loudness of the Doctor's voice was too much for their sensitive ears to bear.

'We must . . . decide . . . what we shall do,' the second Sensorite said, and with his companion moved swiftly out of the room. As they left, Susan closed the door behind them. The Doctor watched the departing aliens with interest: so, they weren't all-powerful after all . . .

'What did they mean, "decide"?' asked Barbara.

'Sounds as if there's something else they can do to us,' suggested Ian ominously.

The Doctor looked thoughtfully at his granddaughter. She had emerged from her dazed state the instant the Sensorites had left the flight deck. 'They might have been referring to Susan,' he said. 'Your mind is particularly sensitive, my child. The Sensorites only spoke to you this time. Next time – if there is a next time – they might try to control your mind.'

'Isn't there any way you can get into your ship, Doctor?' asked an anxious Maitland.

The Doctor shook his head. 'Not until they return what is mine.'

'But they might never give it back to you,' said Carol.

The Doctor smiled at her. 'Then we shall have to take it

51

from them, shan't we? They're not invincible!' He addressed the rest of his companions: 'They seem to find loud noises uncomfortable, for one thing. And another: did any of you notice the pupils of their eyes?'

They all shook their heads.

'They're very large,' said the old man. 'Even in here they were fully dilated to receive as much light as possible.'

'What on Earth are you getting at, Doctor?' asked Ian.

'It's a fallacy that cats can see in the dark; they just see better than humans because the iris of their eyes dilate at night,' explained the Doctor. 'Now, the Sensorites' eyes are the exact opposite of a cat's . . .'

'So the Sensorites' eyes would contract in the darkness?' concluded Ian.

'Exactly! And that is our best weapon – the Sensorites would be frightened in the dark!'

It was the greatest fear of all, but Barbara was not convinced. 'How can you be sure that the Sensorites would be, well, scared of the dark?' she asked.

'My dear Barbara,' said the Doctor, 'wouldn't you be afraid if you couldn't see your enemies?'

Neither Ian nor Barbara needed to consider their answer. They each remembered far too well the terror they had felt in the ship's darkened corridors when they were searching for the Sensorites. In the dark they had been totally helpless, frightened out of their wits. Barbara also remembered something Ian had said earlier: both the humans and the Sensorites were scared stiff of each other.

Pleased with his deductions, the Doctor looked at Ian with a merry twinkle in his eyes. 'Thank you for your admiration, my boy.'

Ian was staggered. 'I never said a word!' he protested.

'Telepathy isn't just a prerequisite of the Sensorites,' said the old man. 'I know sometimes what you're thinking!'

Their merriment was short-lived however. '*I won't go!*' Susan suddenly shouted.

'What?'

The Doctor hushed Ian. 'She's in contact with the Sensorites again.' He looked deep into his granddaughter's glazed eyes. 'What is it, my child?' he asked.

Susan raised her hands to her temples to smooth away the tension she felt. 'I . . . I can't hear them very clearly . . .' she said. 'Wait – that's better, there's just one voice now, a very long way off . . .'

'What are they saying?' asked Barbara.

Ignoring her question, Susan continued her mental conversation with the Sensorites.

'All right,' she said reluctantly; 'but none of the others must be harmed.' She turned back to her friends and held out a hand in warning. 'Don't move any of you.'

Her face grim with determination, she crossed over to the main door. It had slid open again and now standing there in the doorway waiting for Susan were the two Sensorites.

Susan looked over at her grandfather. His face was drawn with concern.

'Grandfather, it was the only way,' she cried plaintively. 'They knew I'd agree . . .'

'Agree to what, my child?' the Doctor asked through trembling lips.

There were tears in Susan's eyes as she explained: 'To go down with them to their planet. Otherwise we'll all be killed.'

5

The Quest for Freedom

Susan turned painfully away from the confused faces of her companions and walked through the doorway to join the Sensorites. After the door slid shut on them it was a few moments before Ian broke the stunned silence.

'Come with me, Barbara, we must stop them!'

'No!' protested Carol. 'The Sensorites will harm or kill her if you try to interfere.'

'And if we do nothing she'll die anyway!' Ian exploded, no longer attempting to conceal the antipathy he felt towards the two astronauts. They seemed perfectly content to let the most terrible things happen to them without any attempt at resistance.

Barbara operated the opening mechanism of the door. 'Are we going to try out the Doctor's theory that they can't see in the dark?' she asked.

Ian nodded. It was the only thing they had to fight the Sensorites with. As the two teachers passed through the doorway in pursuit of Susan and her alien escorts, Barbara glanced back at the Doctor who had remained strangely silent.

The old man was standing there, a strange look of hurt bewilderment in his eyes. Barbara had known the Doctor long enough to guess the cause. Beneath the Doctor's hard shell he was in truth a deeply compassionate and caring man. And the person he cared most for in all the worlds he had ever visited was his granddaughter Susan. And now she had been taken from him. For the first time in his life he felt utterly and completely alone. Shaking his head sadly, he followed Ian and Barbara through the doorway.

When the door had hissed open, Susan and the Sensorites had turned around to see Ian and Barbara coming after them down the corridor.

'Go back!' Susan begged them. 'Don't interfere – please.'

'The young girl has agreed to go with us,' said the first Sensorite. 'She will not be harmed. Why then do you follow us?'

'She must not go with you,' Barbara said firmly, taking a step towards the Sensorites.

'Do not come any nearer!' the first Sensorite commanded and raised his hand weapon in Barbara's direction.

Ian put a restraining hand on Barbara's shoulder, and addressed the aliens. 'We want to talk to you,' he said.

'We have no wish to harm you in any way,' the second Sensorite insisted.

'I said talk – not fight,' countered Ian.

'Intruders from other planets always say that they wish to talk but all they mean to do is to destroy.'

Susan finally spoke for herself and pleaded with Ian: 'Please let me go with them. Because I can use telepathy they trust me.'

'You're not going with them, Susan, and that's final!' snapped Barbara, suddenly back in the classroom.

'Why not?' Susan was defiant. 'It's suspicion that's making them hostile. You don't understand the Sensorites.'

'You think *I* don't understand?' demanded the Doctor, marching purposefully up to the little group. 'Trust is a two-sided affair. If you go with them, they will have all the advantages,' he pointed out.

'They only want to talk to me, Grandfather.'

The Doctor regarded his granddaughter with tenderness, but the tone he took with her was stern. 'I'm sorry, Susan, but I don't believe you have the ability to represent us.'

Susan's patience finally broke. 'Stop treating me like a child!' she cried, so loudly that the Sensorites were once again forced to cover up their ears.

'You will do as you're told, Susan!' barked the Doctor. 'Come here.' He held out a beckoning hand towards her.

'I'm sorry, Grandfather, I can't do it . . .'

'*This instant!*'

Shocked by her grandfather's anger, Susan automatically took a step towards him. Then she checked herself, seeming to weigh up the choices before her: to follow through with her own decision and go with the Sensorites, or to obey without question the man she loved and trusted above all else.

With some reluctance she finally went meekly over to her grandfather's side. The Doctor placed a possessive arm about her shoulder, relieved to have won back his granddaughter from the Sensorites.

As one of the aliens raised its hand weapon in a threatening gesture, the Doctor called out a command to Ian. Suddenly the half-light of the passageway was transformed into near-pitch darkness as Ian activated a light control on the wall. Confused and terrified in the sudden darkness the Sensorites fell wailing to their knees.

'You were absolutely right, Doctor,' said Ian, 'they're helpless in the dark.'

As their eyes quickly grew accustomed to the dark the time-travellers watched in sober reflection as the Sensorites sprawled on the floor, pleading pathetically with Ian to switch on the light. The Doctor instructed Susan to join the others on the flight deck and then told Ian to return the corridor to its usual state of half-illumination. He looked down at the Sensorites who were beginning to struggle to their feet.

'You could have been left here in the darkness,' he said. 'We have proved our power over you but we don't intend to use it – except in our own defence.'

'What do you want of us?' the Sensorites asked.

'Nothing that isn't ours. You stole the lock from my Ship.'

The Sensorites looked at each other in mute communication, and then turned back to the Doctor. 'I must refer this matter to the Sense-Sphere,' the first Sensorite said, moving slightly apart from the humans and his companion. He placed the white disc against his forehead.

The Doctor tapped his foot irritably.

'You must have patience,' the other Sensorite advised. 'The Sense-Sphere is very far away. The mind transmitter amplifies our thoughts. Please have patience.'

The Doctor shot him a look so withering that a charging rhinoceros would have had cause for concern. 'If they try anything, put the light out again,' he told Ian and Barbara. 'I won't put up with this nonsense: dictated to by petty thieves *and* my own grandchild!' And with that he stalked off in the direction of the flight deck.

Barbara watched him go. 'I've never seen him so angry before,' she said to Ian.

'Susan set him off,' he replied. 'The Sensorites must have hypnotised her.'

Barbara smiled. 'No, I don't think so . . . She's just growing up, that's all . . .'

In a quiet corner of the flight deck, away from the ears of Maitland and Carol, the Doctor held his granddaughter affectionately in his arms.

'Now, what is all this?' he asked. 'Setting yourself up against me?'

'I didn't, Grandfather . . .' Susan began to protest.

'I think I'm the best judge of that, Susan,' said the Doctor, some of his former sternness returning to his voice.

Susan raised her head to meet her grandfather's gaze. 'I have opinions too,' she argued.

'My dear girl, the purpose of growing old is to accumulate knowledge and wisdom and to help other people,' the Doctor declared loftily. He sounded exactly like the Victorian headmaster of an English public school.

'So, I'm to be treated like a little child!' said Susan, breaking away from her grandfather's embrace.

'If you behave like one – yes!' he snapped back.

Stuggling to remain calm Susan pleaded with the Doctor. 'I understand the Sensorites,' she said. 'They're really very timid little people. Because my mind and theirs can sometimes communicate they trust me.'

'I assure you we will make use of that fact,' the Doctor promised her. 'But not without discussion. You will not make decisions on your own accord. Is that quite clear?'

Susan took a deep breath: 'I won't be pushed aside, Grandfather. I'm not a child anymore.'

Unnoticed by the Doctor and Susan, the Sensorites had entered the flight deck with Ian and Barbara. They had been listening with interest to the conversation.

'Why do you make her unhappy?' the first Sensorite asked the Doctor.

'We can read the misery in her mind,' the other explained.

Grateful for an opportunity to attack an opponent with

some verbal abuse, the Doctor turned savagely on the two aliens. 'It's a good thing you can't read the anger in my mind,' he began, deliberately raising his voice. 'In all the years my granddaughter and I have been travelling we have never had an argument. And now you creatures have caused one!'

Susan urged him to be silent. 'I'll do as you tell me, Grandfather,' she promised. 'I'll stay with you.'

Caught off-guard, the Doctor was for once lost for words. Eventually he managed to say, 'Very well – now let's work together and get back the lock of the TARDIS.'

'We have orders from the First Elder, our leader,' the first Sensorite said. 'We are to listen to you and transmit your words to him.'

The Doctor once more appointed himself the spokesman for his and Maitland's crew. 'I'm afraid that isn't good enough: I would like to talk to the First Elder face-to-face,' he said. 'I want to arrange the release of this spaceship.' The first Sensorite held his mind transmitter to his forehead, sending the Doctor's words back to the Sense-Sphere as the Doctor continued: 'Tell him we're not pirates or plunderers. There's only one treasure we desire from him: freedom!'

Carol sat on the edge of John's bed, looking down sadly at the sleeping form of the disturbed mineralogist. As if to reassure herself of the presence of the man she loved she affectionately caressed his cheek.

Suddenly he sat bolt upright, his eyes staring ahead with fear.

Carol took him by the shoulders and gently pushed him back down on the bed; just as she would to a child who had woken up from a terrible nightmare.

'It's all right, John,' she whispered comfortingly, 'I'm here.'

She searched in his eyes for a glimmer of recognition, some acknowledgement that he remembered who she was. 'John . . . do you know who I am?' she asked. She silently prayed for the answer she most desired.

John looked searchingly at her, trying to put a name to the face he was sure he knew so well. All he could remember was that this strangely familiar woman was a friend.

'You're . . . you're good,' he said after some hesitation.

Carol turned away as tears welled up in her eyes. John sat up, concerned that he had made his friend cry. 'The Sensorites . . .' he began apologetically. 'They want me to forget . . . all the voices in my head, begging me to forget . . .'

The cabin door slid softly open and Maitland entered. He regarded John with a forced smile and then looked enquiringly at Carol.

'It's no use,' she despaired, 'He might as well be dead . . .' Maitland protested, but she continued, no longer bothering to hold back her tears. 'Can you imagine what it's like to be in love with someone and to stand helplessly by while they're being slowly destroyed?' she sobbed.

Maitland knelt down by her side and clasped her hands in his. 'Carol, the Doctor's been talking to the Sensorites. You're to go down to the Sense-Sphere with John and the others. The Sensorites are going to cure him.'

But Carol was beyond all hope. 'Undo the damage they've caused, you mean,' she said bitterly. 'Can't you see? It's too late.'

After a lengthy discussion between the Doctor and the First Elder, or rather between the Doctor and the Sensorite who relayed his demands to his leader, it had been decided that the time-travellers would be allowed to go down to the Sense-Sphere and negotiate for the return of the TARDIS lock, and the release of Maitland's spaceship.

To prove their good faith the Sensorites had agreed to introduce John to their scientists who would attempt to cure him. In return, Barbara and Maitland were to remain on board the spaceship as hostages in the company of an armed Sensorite warrior.

As the TARDIS crew, Carol and John and their Sensorite escort prepared to leave the spaceship and board the shuttle craft which had been sent up from the Sense-Sphere, one of the Sensorites took the Doctor aside.

'Ten years ago, five humans landed on the Sense-Sphere,' he began tentatively. The Doctor urged him to continue.

'Our planet welcomed them. Their minds were closed against us, but we sensed they thought our planet was a rich one; slowly we began to feel the greed in their hearts as they longed to exploit our mineral wealth.

'Then the five men quarrelled. Two of them took off in their ship which exploded a mile in the atmosphere.'

'What happened to the others?' asked the Doctor.

'We imagined they hid themselves aboard and fought for control of the ship. Anyway, all were killed.'

'My dear sir, I can assure you that we have no intention of robbing you of your precious molybdenum if that's what concerns you,' repeated the Doctor.

'That is good,' said the Sensorite. 'But ever since that day our people have been dying in greater numbers each year, stricken by some unknown disease.'

Ian had joined the Doctor and the Sensorite. 'Could it have been caused by radioactive fall-out from the rocket?' he suggested.

'Perhaps: the power source of their ship was of a type unknown to us. Our people are dying: soon the Sensorite Nation will be no more . . .' The Sensorite diplomatically approached the point of his speech: 'The First Elder says that he senses great wisdom in you, Doctor . . .'

The Doctor crowed with satisfaction. '*I* sense some bargaining ahead of us,' he said. 'I take it you will only accede to our demands when I can find a cure for this disease. Is that so?'

The Sensorite nodded.

'Very well then.' The Doctor agreed: in truth he had no choice. He crossed over to Barbara. 'Reluctant as I am to leave you, my dear, I'm afraid we have no alternative,' he said.

Barbara smiled. 'I'll be all right,' she reassured him. 'I'm just worried about you.'

'Oh, I dare say I'll manage . . .' he boasted. 'Now, come along, Susan, Chesterton.' He beckoned his companions to follow him and marched away toward the spaceship's docking bay.

As the Doctor's party made their way to the awaiting Sensorite ship, Barbara and Maitland waved them goodbye

61

under the watchful eye of their Sensorite guard.

Despite the Doctor's assurances, Barbara felt distinctly uneasy. If the Doctor could not find a cure for the disease that was killing the Sensorites what would happen to them all? Without the TARDIS they would be trapped forever in this forgotten corner of time and space with no chance of ever returning home. Or perhaps the Sensorites would kill them, not prepared to let them stand by as their race died off one by one? Or perhaps they too would fall victim to the disease that was ravaging the Sense-Sphere?

All their fates rested with the Doctor, as they had done so many times before. But could even the Doctor save an entire race from extinction?

6

Hidden Danger

Bounded to the north and west by a range of yellow mountains, and to the south and east by a great blue lake and a lush forest, the Sensorites' City was a haven of beauty and serenity. The sun sparkled down on the domed buildings and crystalline towers of the City, which in turn reflected the sun's light in a thousand different colours. Here and there in secluded gardens Sensorites would stop to talk, their conversations uninterrupted save for the noise of cascading fountains, and the gentle songs of birds.

Most magnificent of all the buildings in the City was the Palace of the Elders, a brilliant blue crystal dome, built on massive arches and towers, and soaring above all else in the City. It was here in this Palace in a small simply furnished chamber at the very apex of the dome that the First and Second Elders of the Sensorite Nation were seated in discussion. The subject of their conversation was the imminent arrival of the Doctor and his party.

The physical appearance of the two Sensorite leaders was almost identical. Apart from the two black sashes which the First Elder wore criss-crossed across his chest, and the single sash worn by the Second Elder, they were virtually indistinguishable.

Hovering around the First Elder's splendid golden throne and hanging on to his two superiors' every word was the City Administrator, a small dumpy Sensorite distinguishable by the black band around his neck. From time to time other Sensorites would enter the chamber, bringing flasks of sparkling water and bowls of fruit.

'Why should we welcome to our planet the same creatures who have been the cause of our destruction?' The Second Elder wanted to know. 'The deaths of our people will increase if these humans are allowed on the Sense-Sphere.'

'I am the ruler of this planet, and I have decided to use the humans to investigate the deaths of our people,' the First Elder declared firmly. 'Sometimes we must fight fire with fire . . .'

'The First Elder makes a wise decision,' ingratiated the Administrator. Neither the First nor the Second Elder paid him an attention.

'These Earth-creatures are loud and ugly things,' continued the Second Elder. 'Why could we not meet them in the desert or the mountains?'

'It is the failure of all beings that they judge through their own eyes,' the First Elder answered patiently. 'To them, we may appear ugly.' The Administrator let out an involuntary gasp of astonishment as the First Elder continued: 'What we must cultivate between ourselves is trust: that is why I have invited them to the Palace.'

'There are animals in our deserts and forests, but we do not invite them into our palaces,' argued the Second Elder. 'How can we be sure that these Earth-creatures are not animals also?'

'Do not underestimate them!' cautioned the First Elder. 'Do we possess a ship that can traverse the borders of the Universe?' he asked, standing up and moving over to a circular table upon which lay a short metallic cylinder – the TARDIS lock. 'This strange mechanism my Warriors brought to me looks like an ordinary lock, but our research proves it to be in reality an electronic miracle which reveals a mind of science far beyond our own.

'It belongs to the one known as the Doctor. *His* mind was quick to realise our weakness in the dark and to use it against us – but not unfairly, merely to protect the girl called Susan. I sense great wisdom and compassion in him; perhaps he can help us where our own scientists have failed.'

The First Elder finally acknowledged the fawning presence of his Administrator and asked for his opinion on the matter.

'Sir, you were elected to lead our people because of your great brain,' he gushed. 'I would not dare to question your actions.'

The First Elder's tone was critical. 'Sometimes no opinion can be worse than a very dogmatic one,' he said, leaving the chamber and taking the TARDIS lock with him.

As the door closed on the Sensorite leader the Second Elder looked curiously at the Adminstrator. 'You need not fear me,' he reassured him. 'You may speak your mind.'

The Administrator approached him with the air of a conspirator. 'You are his second opinion, yet he makes his decision without consulting you . . .' he began cunningly, playing on the Second Elder's ego.

'He makes a wise decision.'

'But based on trust! Do *you* trust these Earth-creatures?'

The Second Elder turned away, unwilling to answer the question. 'The decision of the First Elder cannot be set aside,' he said loyally.

'I would not suggest such a thing,' the Administrator lied. 'But his mind is pure – naive. *We* are realists.' He took a long breath before saying, 'That is why I have beamed the Disintegrator into this room.'

'Without permission!' cried the Second Elder, evidently greatly shocked. 'You are being presumptuous!'

'I am the City Administrator. It is my duty to protect the City and the One Who Rules. If the Earth-creatures use force or commit one suspicious action, the Disintegrator will eradicate them.'

The Second Elder regarded his junior thoughtfully. He did not trust the Earth-creatures as did the First Elder, and perhaps there was some justification for the Administrator's action. After all, the Earth-creatures were aliens: who could know what their motives might be?

Finally he said, 'Very well. But you will do nothing until I have considered the matter fully.' He walked slowly out of the room.

As he did so the Administrator called after him: 'I am acting for the good of the Sensorite Nation. We shall not be safe until these Earth-creatures are dead!'

The journey down from Maitland's ship to the Sense-Sphere had been swift. Despite their fascination with the City's dazzling beauty the Doctor's party were relieved when they finally reached the enclosed forecourt of the Palace of the Elders. Throughout the short trip from the shuttle landing bay to the Palace they had been the subject of wary stares from passing Sensorites who backed away at their approach. It was exactly as if they had the plague, thought the Doctor, and then realised that that was precisely what the Sensorites believed. He made his feelings known to the Sensorite Warrior who had escorted them down to the planet.

'Earth people are not . . . popular,' he agreed. 'They fear that you may bring disease and death to our people.'

'We must explain to them that this disease – if that's what it is – is nobody's fault,' advised the Doctor. 'And besides, there are cures and remedies for every malady.'

The Sensorite indicated his agreement, but then wagged a finger of warning at the Doctor. 'Let the Elders explain this to the people,' he said. 'You are forbidden to talk to the lower castes.'

Susan raised an eyebrow of surprise. 'Lower castes?' she asked. 'Do you have such distinctions?'

'Of course,' said the Warrior, as surprised at Susan's question as she was at him. 'How else can we tell what each is best fitted to do? The Elders think and rule, the Warriors fight, and the Sensorites work and play.'

The Doctor chuckled to himself, rather glad that Barbara was not here. She would have had a few things to say about this over-simplistic view of a well-ordered society.

'All are happy . . .' protested the Sensorite, anticipating Susan's objections.

'. . . but some are happier than others,' finished Ian, amused in spite of himself at the Sensorites' naivety.

'I do not understand,' their escort pursued. 'There is no disgrace in being a member of one of the lower castes. It is simply what one is best fitted to do.'

They approached the inner building of the Palace and the Warrior led them into a lift to take them up to the Chamber of the First Elder. As he did so, John clutched at Carol's arm, breaking the silence he had kept ever since landing on the Sense-Sphere.

'They're near us now,' he said fearfully. 'I can feel an evil mind . . .'

Carol started to question him further, but Susan stopped her. 'His mind is open: he can tell the difference between good and evil people,' she reminded her, and then looked at the disturbed astronaut. 'What is it, John? What are you trying to tell us?'

But John was silent again, unable to put into words the anxieties he felt in his mind. As he and the two girls followed the others into the lift, a figure emerged from his hiding place behind the greenery. His fears confirmed, the City Administrator rushed down one of the walkways to the Disintegrator Room.

These creatures were dangerous: it was time to destroy them.

The Disintegrator Room was located almost directly underneath the Palace of the Elders, and formed part of the Science Block where Sensorite scientists and engineers busied themselves in their appointed tasks.

The Disintegrator itself was a huge complex of computer banks and consoles, capable of beaming a ray of white hot energy to any point in the City. A remnant of the Sensorites' warring past, it had been carefully preserved and was still kept in a state of permanent maintenance. It was now used primarily as an excavating machine: its carefully precisioned laser could cut through solid rock more easily than any conventional tool.

As the Administrator entered the room a Sensorite engineer acknowledged his presence and stood to attention.

'Is all prepared?' the Administrator asked his accomplice.

The Engineer nodded towards the main control console of the Disintegrator. 'All I need is the Firing Key.'

The Administrator handed him a long transparent plastic tube, filled with intricate microcircuitry. The Engineer took it from him and inserted it into a purpose-built socket on the console. The unit immediately buzzed into life.

'The Disintegrator ray must be beamed directly on the Chamber of the First Elder,' instructed the Administrator, and handed the Engineer five strips of punched plastic. 'Five places have been assigned to the Earth-creatures; these are the co-ordinates. In each case you must aim at their hearts: that way we can be sure of eradicating them.'

The Engineer fed the five plastic strips into a slot at the side of the machine, and then drew his superior's attention to a small video screen on the unit. Across the screen moved five green dots: the thermal traces of the Doctor, Ian, Susan, Carol and John. 'The Disintegrator is now beamed and ready,' he said. 'Once the Earth-creatures enter the room and take their positions I shall fire.'

The minutes passed slowly as the Administrator and the Engineer tracked the five moving blips on the screen and watched them eventually enter the Chamber of the First Elder. The points of light stopped for a moment and then the two representing John and Carol separated themselves from the others and moved off screen. Puzzled, the Engineer looked up to the Administrator for instruction. He urged him to continue: they would destroy the three aliens in the chamber first, and John and Carol later.

Suddenly an authoritative and indignant voice broke into their concentration. 'Stop! Disconnect the Disintegrator at once!'

The two Sensorites turned around to see the Second Elder standing in the doorway. The veins at his temples were pounding with outrage.

'Why?' demanded the Administrator, silently cursing the Second Elder. 'They are Earth-creatures and therefore dangerous to us.'

'No. They are civilised beings. They are talking to the First Elder in a most friendly fashion. The First Elder has already agreed to cure the man known as John. We need not fear them.'

'The trust we give to each other we cannot give to the Earth-creatures,' protested the Administrator. 'They are aliens: they threaten our entire way of life.'

The Second Elder ignored him and demanded the Firing Key of the Disintegrator. He held out his hand to the Engineer who had remained in shaken silence throughout. Such was the authority in the Second Elder's voice and bearing that the Engineer could not refuse.

'I will place this in the safekeeping of the Chief of Warriors,' the Second Elder said as he took the Key.

Clutching the Firing Key in his hand he turned to go; but before he left the room he addressed the Administrator. 'I am doubtful about you,' he said. 'Do not let my doubts become a reality.'

As the door closed behind him, the Administrator turned furiously to his accomplice. The Second Elder's humiliation of him in front of his servant would not go unavenged.

'We are being bound hand and foot and given to these Earth-creatures,' he said. There was no mistaking the hate in his voice. 'Our leaders have grown weak.'

'I will follow you,' volunteered the Engineer. 'I do not trust these creatures either.'

'I am grateful for your loyalty,' said the Administrator sincerely. 'The First and Second Elders have let themselves be deceived. If they do not change their attitudes they may have to give way to another Sensorite of stronger thought.' It was obvious who he thought that Sensorite should be.

The Engineer pressed his fist to his chest in an oath of allegiance. 'Command me,' he said.

'Have patience,' the Administrator advised him. 'The time for action will not be far away . . .'

The First Elder had greeted the Doctor's party with great cordiality and, as the Second Elder had revealed, had readily agreed to the Doctor's request that John be treated by the Sensorite scientists. However, declared the Doctor, that did not alter the fact that the Sensorites were responsible for his condition in the first place.

Before explaining his actions the First Elder urged them all to sit down and called for refreshments. As if from nowhere, Sensorite servants appeared, bringing with them plates piled with exotic fruits. Ian noted with some astonishment that the plates were made of solid gold.

Satisfied that his guests were well provided for, the First Elder began his story: 'John was like the other humans who came here ten years ago. When he discovered that our planet was rich in molybdenum his mind just opened up to us. We were able to see the pictures in his mind: he dreamt of a fleet of spaceships coming to mine our metal and transport it back to Earth. It would have been the end of our way of life. We had no alternative but to imprison him and his friends in orbit above the Sense-Sphere.'

'That's still no reason for driving him out of his mind,' Ian insisted as he munched thoughtfully on a peach-like fruit.

The Sensorite raised a hand in protest. 'That was . . . unfortunate. It happened because his excitement opened up his mind. The others fell into a deep sleep, as we planned, but he heard the full power of our voices in his brain. His mind had no reserve, no defence . . . We had no wish to harm anyone at all: that is not our way. Please believe me.'

As the Doctor, Ian and Susan realised that they might have misjudged the Sensorites after all, another servant entered the room. He carried on a tray goblets of sparkling water. Ian looked wonderingly at the drinking vessels: they looked suspiciously as if they were fashioned from pure platinum.

As the Doctor raised a goblet to his lips, the First Elder stopped him and angrily rose from his seat and turned to his servant. 'Why do you insult our guests?' he demanded. 'Why do you not give them the same water as you give me? You will bring them the crystal water immediately!' With a wave of his hand he dismissed his servant who scuttled off muttering his apologies.

Amused at the First Elder's anxiety to ensure that his guests had the best of everything, Ian asked, 'Crystal water? What's the difference between that and ordinary water?'

'In the Yellow Mountains I discovered a pure spring, the water of which I believe to hold special qualities,' their host explained. 'I have flagons of it stored for the exclusive use of the Elders. We are very proud of our aqueduct,' he added. 'It lies beneath the City at the foot of the Mountains.'

Ian grinned. 'Well, I hope you don't mind if I have some of this ordinary water while I'm waiting. I'm very thirsty.' He picked up a goblet and sipped at the water, smiling in appreciation as he felt the cool liquid run down his throat.

Impatient with this polite display of good manners and gastronomical discussion the Doctor typically came straight to the point.

'Now, my good sir,' he said to the First Elder, 'we were brought here to find a cure for this mysterious disease of yours. In return, you will give back to us the lock of my Ship and return these unfortunate spacepeople home. Am I right?'

'That is so,' the First Elder said as he waved his servant back into the room. He was now bearing goblets filled with the crystal water.

'Would you tell us something about the disease?' Ian asked as he passed a plate of fruit to Susan. Suddenly he began to cough and splutter, and Susan put down her fruit to give him a hearty pat on the back.

'The disease resists all our attempts to stamp it out,' explained the First Elder. 'It hits all manner of our people, irrespective of their caste.'

'Including the Elders?' asked the Doctor.

The First Elder shook his head. 'No. So far it seems we have been fortunate.'

'Do you think there might be a clue there, Doctor?' asked Ian, who began to launch into a fit of hacking coughs.

'My dear Chesterton,' said the Doctor, 'are you all right?'

Susan pressed a hand against Ian's forehead. It was covered in sweat. His face too had taken on a sudden deathly pallor.

The Doctor looked enquiringly at the First Elder. 'Is this a symptom of your disease?' he asked.

'My throat's burning,' Ian gasped. He tried to stand up on shaking legs, but the whole world was spinning sickeningly about him. He collapsed on the floor, sending his drink and food on the table before him flying in all directions.

Susan knelt down to him, instinctively feeling for his pulse. She looked up, concerned, at her grandfather and the First Elder who were standing over her. 'He's unconscious, Grandfather. His pulse is racing ahead . . .'

The First Elder looked sadly down at Ian's trembling body. With genuine regret he said, 'There is no hope. Your friend is dying . . .'

7

A Race Against Death

Ian lay writhing on the floor of the chamber, his body and clothes soaked in sweat. The Doctor, Susan and the First Elder bent over him in concern. As the Doctor mopped Ian's brow with his pocket handkerchief he marvelled at the incredible build-up in his companion's body temperature.

'This disease of yours, is it contagious?' he asked the distressed First Elder.

The Sensorite shook his head. 'No, but it strikes indiscriminately at our people and without warning.'

'Now, that is unusual,' remarked the Doctor. 'I wonder, could it be a germ in the air . . .'

Susan looked anxiously at her grandfather. 'Grandfather, it doesn't seem like a disease at all, does it?' she said, echoing the old man's thoughts. 'If Ian's got it why haven't we? We've done everything together; gone down from the spaceship, come here . . . What about the fruit?'

The Doctor stood up and stroked his chin. 'No,' he said, 'you had some of that too . . .'

Suddenly a spark of triumph flashed in his eyes. 'I know! Ian drank a different kind of water! And that would explain why the Elders are unaffected: they drink only the crystal water!'

The First Elder was puzzled. 'But why do not all those who drink the ordinary water die? It all comes from the same source.'

The Doctor brushed his question aside. 'It depends on their resistance,' he surmised. 'But in due course all will die.'

'Are you sure of this?'

'Of course I'm not sure – yet,' the Doctor replied tartly. 'But for the moment that's all we have to go on. Now, please call for a servant.'

The First Elder complied with the request. Susan called her grandfather's attention back to Ian. His eyes had now reopened and he was groaning in pain, clutching at his stomach. The Doctor bent down to comfort him.

'This isn't a disease – it's more like a poison,' he muttered to himself while feeling for Ian's pulse. He looked up as the Sensorite servant entered the room. 'Go to your scientists,' he ordered. 'I want some sodium chloride and I want it immediately.'

The servant looked at the First Elder for confirmation and then scurried out of the chamber.

The Sensorite leader made his concern known to the Doctor; he offered to do all in his power to help the old man and see that Ian was cured.

'For a start you can ensure that no one drinks anything but the crystal water,' began the Doctor. 'Secondly, I must work with your scientists. I presume you have a laboratory in the Palace?'

The First Elder nodded.

Susan stood up, leaving Ian who had once more lapsed into unconsciousness. She walked over to her grandfather. 'How long has he got?' she asked in a broken whisper.

To her surprise it was the First Elder who answered her question. 'I hear the distress in your mind and I respond to it,' he sympathised. 'From the first signs no one has lived longer than the third day.'

Susan looked aghast; but the Doctor beamed. 'As long as that?' he asked jubilantly. 'Then we have more time!' He took the First Elder aside and said confidentially to him, 'Sir, I have chemicals on board my Ship, the TARDIS. Return the lock to me and I shall not only cure my young friend, but save your entire race!'

The First Elder regarded the old man with suspicion. Was this merely some ruse to regain the lock of the TARDIS? Could the Doctor really be trusted? 'I must discuss this matter with the Second Elder,' he stalled.

'Very well,' the Doctor conceded reluctantly. 'But do not delay one second longer than you have to!'

The First Elder bowed in agreement and left the chamber, just as a Sensorite servant entered carrying a golden platter piled high with salt.

Taking the platter off him the Doctor tipped the salt into

one of the goblets of crystal water and stirred the solution with a pencil he took out of his jacket pocket.

Motioning Susan to raise Ian's head he passed the bowl to the schoolteacher's lips. As Ian opened his eyes the Doctor smiled encouragingly at him.

'Now, I want you to drink this, my boy,' he said, sounding just like an old-fashioned family doctor. 'It's not going to be pleasant, but it's all for your own good.'

As Ian sipped at the salt and water solution his face screwed up in disgust, but Susan urged him on, and within a minute he had drained the goblet of its unsavoury contents. Seconds later he began to cough and retch, spitting up green vomit. Susan turned her head away in distaste.

Concerned as he was with Ian and this primitive attempt to purge his system, the Doctor's thoughts were now elsewhere – with the First and Second Elders. If they decided not to allow him access to the TARDIS there was no guarantee that he could save Ian's life – or find a cure for the mysterious disease that was killing the Sensorites. And if he could not cure the Sensorites, they might soon all wish that they were dead . . .

In a secluded garden near the Palace, with a magnificent view of the Yellow Mountains, the First and Second Elders were engaged in a heated discussion over the future of the TARDIS crew.

The First Elder felt instinctively that the TARDIS lock ought to be returned to the Doctor. But to justify such a controversial action to his people he needed the advice and support of his chief advisor. And what concerned the First Elder most of all was not that his deputy was against such a course of action, but that he was voicing many of the First Elder's own private fears and doubts.

'The Doctor may not be sincere,' the Second Elder warned. 'He says his friend is dying – but who is to say that he is not pretending? Once we let him into his ship who knows what power he may use to bring us to his mercy? They may go away and return with an army of human beings in a fleet of spaceships and destroy our way of life forever . . .'

'This is a terrible picture you paint,' the First Elder sighed.

'Do you mistrust them as much as all that?'

'I do not trust them . . . as much as you . . .' The Second Elder chose his words carefully. 'They are different from us – alien beings from another world. Their kind have brought only disease and despair to the Sensorite Nation. What basis do we have for trusting them?'

The First Elder considered his junior thoughtfully. The arguments he had presented disturbed him deeply. 'I will reflect upon your advice, and weigh up the matter,' he promised.

'As you will, sir,' the Second Elder replied as his leader left the garden. 'But in all dealings with these aliens I advise caution – extreme caution . . .'

In one of the laboratories in the Science Block John had been strapped down to a large chair. His head was covered with a kind of skull cap, attached to which were hundreds of tiny electrodes which were in turn connected to a large bank of instrumentation at the far end of the room. Periodically his eyes would flicker open and shut, and even after a few hours on the Sensorites' mind restorer his face appeared more relaxed. A few streaks of black now ran through his white hair.

Making delicate adjustments to a control unit at John's side was the Sensorites' Senior Scientist. On his grey tunic he wore a vertical black band around which coiled a spiral design. As the City Administrator entered the room, the Scientist bowed low, affording him the respect due to his caste.

'What is happening here?' asked the senior Sensorite.

'I am clearing the Earthman's mind,' explained the Scientist, discreetly adding, 'On the orders of the First Elder.'

The Administrator regarded John with barely disguised contempt. 'It would have been better to kill him than cure him,' he sneered.

'Once again you question the voice of authority.'

The Administrator spun quickly round to see the Second Elder, recently returned from his meeting with the First Elder, enter the room. He dismissed the Senior Scientist.

Recovering his composure, the Administrator explained

76

himself: 'I am responsible for the safety of this City and I will do anything in my power to defend it from the aliens.'

'Be careful that your power is not taken from you,' the Second Elder advised him. 'Whether you like it or not the man called John is to be cured: we fulfil our promise.'

'Any moment now you will put them in their ship and let them go,' mocked the Administrator.

'One more insolent word from you and I shall demand that your collar of office be taken from you,' said the Second Elder, pointing to the black band around the Administrator's neck. 'This man is to be cured. As for the other one –'

The Administrator interrupted him. 'Which other one?'

'The one called Ian Chesterton.'

'These absurd names they all have!' scoffed the Administrator. 'They bear no badges of authority or position. How are we to distinguish them? They all look the same . . . What is the matter with the other one?'

'He has contracted the disease. But their commander, the Doctor, believes our water supply is to blame.'

Like someone who has had his most cherished belief suddenly swept away from under him, the Administrator began to clutch at spurious explanations for the Doctor's apparent co-operation. 'A brilliant scheme!' he finally declared with irony. 'There is nothing wrong with our water supply. But by destroying confidence in one of our necessities they hope to bring us to their mercy!'

As the Administrator defended his misguided beliefs, John's eyes slowly opened, and he regarded the Sensorite with a look of fear and recognition.

'Evil . . . evil . . .' he muttered.

The Administrator immediately seized on the astronaut's words. 'Even this half-broken creature here admits the truth! These Earth-creatures are evil – they must not be allowed to undermine the security of our Nation . . .'

The Second Elder looked closely at the Administrator for some long seconds and then turned to go. He had no wish to listen to any more of the Administrator's confused and paranoid prattlings. As he left the room, John cried out, 'No, no! Evil is here!'

The Administrator bowed close to John's ear as the door

closed behind the Second Elder. 'Your mind is closed by the machine,' he whispered. 'You will not be believed.'

Unable to move in the straps which bound him to the chair, John could only look at the Administrator with terror. '*You* are the enemy!' he accused.

'I am the enemy of all Earth-creatures who come to plunder and destroy our planet,' the Administrator declared proudly.

John struggled wildly in his chair but to no avail. So great was his terror before the Sensorite that his mind took the only defence it could. He fainted cold away.

The Administrator looked down at him contemptuously. 'Your primitive mind is too weak to harm me,' he said.

Just then Carol entered the room behind him. Freshly bathed and changed, and with her fair hair let down and falling about her shoulders, she looked far more relaxed than when the TARDIS crew had first encountered her up in Maitland's spaceship. Now that she was free of the Sensorites' mental assaults, and now that there was some hope for John, there was a spring in her step and a smile on her face.

'How's John?' she asked, and then checked herself as the Administrator turned around to face her. 'Oh, I am sorry,' she apologised, 'I thought you were one of the scientists.'

The Administrator's tone was severe. 'Did you not see my collar of office?' he asked, pointing to the black band around his neck.

'I said I'm sorry,' she replied, slightly irritated by the Administrator's attitude. 'When your backs are turned it's very difficult to see who you are.' She chuckled. 'I don't know what we'd do if you all changed your badges and sashes: we wouldn't be able to tell you apart.'

'I had never thought of that before . . .' the Administrator said slowly, struck by the novelty of the idea.

As Carol concerned herself with John, the Administrator walked away pensively. Already a plan was forming in his devious mind . . .

The Doctor was furious. He and Susan had been in the First Elder's Chamber for over an hour, anxiously awaiting the First Elder's decision as to whether they would be allowed entry to the TARDIS. All the while Ian had been moaning deliriously to himself, wracked by excruciating pains on a low couch which had been provided for him. When the First Elder finally returned the Doctor was tapping his coat lapels in irritation, and looked fit to explode.

'Well?' he demanded.

'I am sorry, Doctor,' said the Sensorite leader, 'I cannot allow you to go to your ship.'

'You dare set yourself up against me!' the old man thundered in a voice loud enough to wake the dead. 'I must have the chemicals and equipment; otherwise Chesterton will die and it will be your fault – and yours alone!'

So great was the Doctor's fury that the Sensorite was forced to cover his ears to shut out the painful noise. Susan immediately interposed herself between the two opponents in an attempt to mediate.

'Please, Grandfather,' she pleaded in a soft yet firm voice, 'he thinks you're attacking him. Turning to the Sensorite she explained, 'We're sorry: we don't mean to use sound as a weapon. We don't mean to hurt you.'

'Very well, I accept your apology,' replied the First Elder and then addressed the Doctor once more. 'Please be more careful in future,' he said with veiled sarcasm. The Doctor shot him a glance of pure poison.

'But it is inhuman! Ian will die if we can't help him! he protested in a harsh whisper.

'There is a laboratory in the Palace,' the First Elder reminded him. 'You may prove your theory there.'

'*Theory!*' cried the Doctor indignantly. Susan again urged him to lower his voice as he continued: 'Very well, I realise we have no alternative – but this behaviour is outrageous. Susan, you must stay here with Chesterton. Let him have as much of the crystal water as he wants; and if his breathing gets weak, try artificial respiration.' Turning to the First Elder, he said, 'And now, sir, to your laboratory. And let us just hope that there is still time to save him!'

Even the Doctor had to admit reluctantly that the Palace laboratory was impressive. Small but very comprehensive, it contained an abundance of highly advanced scientific equipment. The Doctor looked on approvingly as the Sensorite scientists busied themselves at their computer banks and work benches with single-minded determination. The Sensorites had developed all the sciences to a high level of sophistication; all, that is, except one, ironically the one they needed most at the moment: for all their intelligence and skill, the Sensorites' knowledge of chemistry was extremely basic.

With his pince-nez glasses perched on his nose, the Doctor addressed the two Sensorite scientists who had been instructed to assist him. The old man was in his element: there was nothing he liked better than showing off his knowledge.

'Now, gentlemen,' he began, like a lecturer in the classroom, 'I believe your people are dying off because there is atropine poisoning in the water.' He took out of his jacket pocket the notebook he always carried with him, and consulted it. 'These are the symptoms: abdominal pains; a sharp rise in bodily temperature, pulse rates become very rapid; a rash may appear; and the mouth and throat become very fiery: exactly the symptoms of our young friend Chesterton. What we have to do, gentlemen, is to establish that this is indeed atropine poisoning, and then prescribe a remedy.'

'But we have already tested the water,' objected the first scientist.

'Then we shall have to try again, shan't we?' the Doctor said. 'The strange thing is that not all of your people have died.'

'Three in every ten,' offered the second scientist. 'Last year it was two in every ten.'

'Of course, some of you may be able to resist it. And pehaps some of the water is good . . .'

'But all the water is the same,' protested the second scientist.

'But surely from different outlets?'

'There are ten Districts in the City – but only one source.'

'Then there definitely is a poison at work. I know the signs,' said the Doctor. 'We must test samples from each and every District. Which District did this one come from?' he asked, taking up a specimen tube of water from the workbench.

'This Palace,' replied the first scientist. 'It is in District

Ten.'

'Then we will test this first – but there's not a moment to lose. I want samples from all the other Districts immediately – it's imperative!'

The Doctor's intention was to test samples of water from each of the reservoirs serving the City's Ten Districts. By adding a specially prepared chemical solution to each of the samples he hoped to detect the presence of atropine poisoning in the water. If poison was present the treated sample would turn dark in colour; if no poison was present it would remain clear.

Hours passed slowly as the Doctor and his two assistants conducted their series of tests on the water samples. From time to time the First or the Second Elder would enter the laboratory to enquire after their progress and bring news of Ian.

Despite all of Susan's attention the schoolteacher was rapidly getting worse. His forehead was bathed in a cold sweat and he was becoming more and more delirious. Each time the Sensorites returned to them Susan would look up anxiously, but each time the only answer they could give her was a sad shake of the head.

Finally after almost five hours of testing and retesting the Doctor turned triumphantly around to his Sensorite helpers. In his right hand he held aloft the specimen tube taken from District Eight: the water inside it had turned a deep black.

'Just as I suspected!' he pronounced. 'Atropine poisoning!'

The Second Elder hurried to the Chamber of the First Elder to break the good news. The Sensorite leader received him with caution. 'Has the Doctor discovered a cure?' he asked.

'He says so: he has identified the poison in our water. Physo-stirate-salicilate' – he pronounced the strange words carefully – 'is the antidote.'

'Remarkable!' rejoiced the First Elder. 'See to it that the antidote is produced in great quantities. Instruct our Senior Scientist to make regular reports on the progress.' Almost as an afterthought he said, 'And convey to the Doctor my congratulations.'

'I will, sir,' said the Second Elder. 'And now I ask to be

excused. I have an appointment with the City Administrator.'

The First Elder dismissed his second-in-command and walked over to Susan who was still nursing the unconscious Ian.

'The Doctor has had some success,' he said softly. 'A remedy will be available soon.'

Susan's tears of relief came quickly. She looked down at Ian's still form. 'Do you hear that, Ian?' she said. 'You're going to be all right.'

The Second Elder had been surprised to receive a request for an audience from the City Administrator. After the happenings of the past few hours he would have thought that he was the last Sensorite he wanted to see. But if the Administrator wished to explain his unruly behaviour the Second Elder would be more than ready to listen; after all, they were still Sensorites.

He was therefore more than a little taken aback when, immediately upon entering the Disintegrator Room, he was violently seized by two Sensorite servants.

The Administrator waddled up to his superior and removed the mind transmitter he always wore at his belt.

'You will be punished for this offence!' snapped the Second Elder, struggling to free himself from the grasp of the two servants.

The Administrator sneered. 'I advise you to co-operate and answer all my questions. Your Family Group is also my prisoner.'

'What have you done with them?' the Second Elder asked fearfully.

'Nothing – so far.' The implication was obvious, as was the Administrator's pleasure in holding at his mercy the one Sensorite who had continually interfered with his plans. 'Has the Doctor completed his experiments?' he asked.

The Second Elder nodded.

'And the antidote is to be given first to the man Ian Chesterton, and then to those of our people who are also ill?'

The Elder confirmed this.

'I do not believe there is an antidote,' said the Administrator. 'The Earth-creature is merely feigning illness. The

Doctor pretends to cure him, and then he will kill us all with the poison he has made in our laboratory.'

'No!' protested his prisoner. 'That is not true. I too had my doubts but our scientists have worked with him and they say –'

'Silence!' The Administrator cut him short. 'You are a traitor to our people. You are not worthy to wear your sash of office.'

As the two servants held the Second Elder, the Administrator took off the single black sash his prisoner wore across his chest. The Second Elder watched aghast, stunned at the Administrator's audacity: the Administrator was taking off his own collar of office and putting on the sash of the office of Second Elder of the Sensorite Nation.

'This so-called antidote must be stopped before it poisons us all,' declared the Administrator. 'The people will obey their Elders.'

'But the First Elder himself has approved the antidote,' protested the Second Elder.

'And yet it will be stopped,' came the reply. 'The Second Elder will stop it!'

'I will not!'

The Administrator's mouth twisted into a sadistic smirk as he delivered his *coup de grâce*.

'I wear your sash of office now. Who is to know that I am not the Second Elder?'

8

Into the Darkness

Carol looked admiringly at the Doctor: she had a lot to thank
him for. Not only had he rescued her from the Sensorites'
mental assaults, teaching her to face her fear rather than hide
from it, but he had also arranged for John's treatment; and
now that he had found a cure for the Sensorites' disease it
seemed that he had even won them back their freedom. He
was quite simply the most extraordinary man she had ever
met.

She wondered just how old he really was. He could deliver
abuse and criticism like any crotchety old man; and the next
moment he would approach a new and apparently insuperable
problem with all the unbridled enthusiasm of a little boy.
Beneath his thick white mane of hair his face was lined and
ancient. But in his firm blue eyes there sparked the mischievous twinkle of youth, like two bright faraway stars in
the night sky at home.

But there was something else in his eyes too, something
which he shared with his granddaughter, Susan. Carol found
it hard to define but it was a deep strangeness, an *other-
worldliness*, something which set them apart from everyone
else. Just who were the Doctor and Susan? Where had they
come from? And, for that matter, where were they going?

Carol smiled at him. 'You're tired out, Doctor,' she said.

'It's a happy tiredness, my dear,' he sighed and eased
himself out of his seat to cross over to where John was still
strapped to the Sensorites' mind restorer, slipping in and out
of consciousness. There were now but a few streaks of white
in the astronaut's otherwise dark hair.

'He's improving,' said Carol in response to the Doctor's
unspoken question. 'But sometimes he goes back to that old
state of confusion.'

'Well, you must expect that. It will take some time but he
will be cured. The mind is a very delicate thing, you know.'

At that moment the Senior Scientist entered the room, holding a jar containing a solution of the antidote. The Doctor uncorked the bottle and took a cursory sniff at the contents.

'Excellent, my friend,' he said to the Senior Scientist. 'Make this up in large quantities and see that all your people who are ill get it. And take this to my granddaughter, Susan.'

'I shall send a messenger immediately,' said the Sensorite and left the room with the bottle.

The Doctor turned back to Carol. 'Now we shall soon be off this planet, my dear, once the Sensorites see the efficacy of my cure.' He rubbed his hands with glee. 'You know, I was rather baffled by this atropine poisoning at first because it only seemed to appear in one part of the City, in one reservoir at a time. It's all very curious . . .'

'But you've discovered an antidote now,' said Carol. 'What's the use of worrying over it?'

'Ah yes, that's a cure – but why cure something when we can stamp it out altogether, hmm?'

Carol was about to question the Doctor further when John distracted her. He was semiconscious and muttering to himself.

She bent down to listen to him: 'Enemy . . . plotting . . .'

'He's more coherent now,' Carol explained, 'but it's as if he were living in a dream where he's surrounded by enemies.'

John was now fully conscious and had caught Carol's words. 'Yes! Enemies, making plots . . .'

The Doctor regarded John thoughtfully, tapping his fingertips together. 'He might be more lucid that you think,' he observed. 'I must leave you now, but I want you to take a careful note of what he says.'

'Where are you going to, Doctor?' asked Carol, surprised at the old man's renewed burst of energy.

'I'm going after the Senior Scientist and then we're setting off on a little expedition. It isn't dangerous of course,' he said hastily in response to Carol's look of concern. 'But when I've solved my problem I'm sure we'll all be out of trouble.'

And without explaining exactly what he meant the Doctor left the room.

On one of the walkways which led from the Palace of the

Elders the City Administrator walked confidently with his collaborator, the Sensorite Engineer. Upon his chest the Administrator wore the sash of the Second Elder.

From time to time Sensorites would pass by them and bow in deference to the Administrator's assumed rank. He smiled and remarked to his assistant, 'My plan is a success. All recognise me as the Second Elder.'

'But what if your disguise is seen through?' asked the nervous Engineer.

'The First and Second Elders are well known only to those in high office,' he explained. 'The lower castes rarely see them except at a distance, and it is to the common folk that I shall expose the true nature of the Earth-creatures' perfidious schemes.'

As a Sensorite scientist rushed past them on his way to the Palace the Administrator commanded him to halt. He was eager to try out his newly acquired status.

'Sensorite, why do you not acknowledge the Second Elder?' he asked.

The scientist bowed respectfully to his superior. 'Forgive me, sir, but I have an urgent appointment with the First Elder in the Palace.' He indicated the glass jar he was carrying. 'The Doctor has found a cure for the poisoning in our water supply. Here is the antidote.'

'You take it to the Earth-creature that is ill?'

'The scientist nodded and the Administrator held out his hand. 'Give the antidote to me. I will deliver it. Return to your duties.'

The scientist complied without question. He had no wish to cross a superior. After he had left, the Administrator turned triumphantly to his accomplice.

'They are trying to poison us all!' he declared. 'They say that without the antidote the young man will die; I say he will live because he merely pretends to be ill. This will prove it one way or another!'

He flung the glass jar to the ground, smashing it into a hundred shimmering pieces. Within minutes the precious antidote had soaked into the ground and was gone.

The Senior Scientist had treated the Doctor's request to see the City's aqueduct with surprise. After some initial protests he had however bowed to the Doctor's new status as an honoured guest of the Sensorite Nation and had led him down to a vast underground cave system near the foot of the Yellow Mountains, some miles out from the City.

Hewn out of the solid rock was an enormous chamber, through which passed massive leaden pipes, carrying water to the ten Districts of the Sensorite City. The contrast between the airy brightness of the Palace of the Elders and the enclosed darkness of the aqueduct was pronounced, a fact the Doctor remarked upon.

'There is some natural phosphorescence in the caves,' explained the Senior Scientist. 'But all our attempts to light the cave and tunnel system artificially have met with failure.'

'That must make it rather difficult for you,' observed the Doctor. 'You Sensorites dislike darkness, don't you?'

'We have no reason to go down the aqueduct anyway,' the Sensorite said defensively.

'Perhaps it's because you've neglected it so long that the waters have become poisoned?' the Doctor supposed, with a hint of disapprobation in his voice.

The Senior Scientist ignored the Doctor's conjecture. 'Shall we return now?' he asked. 'I find the darkness . . . uncomfortable.'

'Return? My dear fellow, I haven't come here just to look – I'm going in there!'

The Scientist was shocked. 'You must not!' he protested. 'You won't be able to see!'

'But I have a torch,' exclaimed the Doctor as he produced a long silver object from the equipment case he was carrying.

'There are monsters . . .' continued the Scientist. 'We have heard them . . .'

'And not seen them?'

'No. But they are there,' he insisted. 'The noise is terrible.'

The Doctor smiled kindly at his companion. 'I think you should return to the laboratory,' he suggested. 'I shall be perfectly safe.'

The Senior Scientist stared at the old man as if he were mad, and then turned gratefully to go, leaving the chamber as fast as his dignity would allow him.

As the Doctor watched him go a theory was already forming in his mind. 'How very convenient,' he reflected to himself. 'Noise and darkness – the two things the Sensorites dislike the most. There's more to this than meets the eye . . .'

He turned to follow the course of the pipelines into the darkness beyond. There in the inky blackness was the source of all the Sensorites' troubles; and no matter what danger lay ahead he was confident that he would soon sort it all out.

The Doctor was enjoying himself immensely.

Back in the Palace Susan was looking down at Ian's smiling face. They had waited over an hour for the Sensorite scientist to bring the antidote, and when he had not arrived the First Elder had sent one of his own servants to fetch another sample from the laboratory. Now some time later Ian was feeling much better although he was still weak and his face was deathly pale.

'I cannot understand why we never received the antidote,' said the First Elder, disturbed.

'We got some in the end though – that's all that really matters,' said Susan, and turned back to Ian. 'Now, there'll be no running about for you for a while,' she teased.

'Yes, Matron,' said Ian, joining in the joke. 'I'm quite happy to stay here.'

The Senior Scientist was announced and when he entered the room the First Elder addressed him sternly. 'I asked for regular reports on the production of the antidote,' he reminded him. 'Why have my orders not been complied with?'

'Forgive me, sir. The Doctor asked me to escort him down to the aqueduct. He said that was where the root of all our trouble lay.'

The First Elder was horrified. 'Did you not warn him?' he asked.

Susan left Ian's bedside and joined the others. 'Warn him of what?' she asked.

'There are monsters in the aqueduct . . .'

'And you let him go down there alone!' Ian was outraged.

'I couldn't stop him,' claimed the Senior Scientist weakly.

'Haven't you got someone you can send down and help him?' Ian asked.

The First Elder came to the defence of his fellow Sensorite. 'The caverns are dark. We are helpless there. Other expeditions have tried to penetrate the blackness and all have failed. Those that return speak of the most terrible things . . .'

'Then I'll have to go myself,' determined Ian, swinging his legs down off the bed and beckoning Susan to help him to his feet.

'You're too ill, Ian,' she protested in vain.

'I'm not that ill,' was the angry retort. 'Anyway we can't stay here.'

Susan gave way to his determination and helped him to stand. As she did so the First Elder pleaded with them: 'If you are resolved to go down to the aqueduct I shall not stop you; the Senior Scientist will arrange transportation and show you the way . . . But I beg you, please change your mind; you cannot save your friend.'

Ian looked incredulously at the First Elder. 'We'll never know till we try, will we!' he shouted, deliberately raising his voice. 'You people amaze me: the Doctor's just saved your people and now you're perfectly happy to let him die! Well, I'm not!' Disgusted, he turned to the Senior Scientist. 'Now, lead the way!'

Susan and the Scientist helped Ian out of the room, leaving the First Elder alone, Ian's voice still pounding painfully in his ears.

The schoolteacher's words had struck home and for the first time the Sensorite leader recognised the true worth of the Earth-creatures. Determining to tell his Second Elder how they had misjudged the humans, he raised his mind transmitter to his forehead . . .

. . . In the Disintegrator Room the Second Elder's hands were tightly bound with plastic wire. Standing gloatingly by the Disintegrator control panel was the City Administrator, still wearing the Second Elder's sash of office.

Suddenly the Second Elder stiffened in his chair as the First Elder's thought waves reached his mind. The Administrator came instantly to his side.

'Some mind is contacting yours,' he said. 'Is it the First

Elder?'

'Give me my mind transmitter,' asked his prisoner.

'Do you think I am a fool?' scoffed the Administrator. 'You can hear but without the mind transmitter your mind cannot speak. What is he saying to you?'

The Second Elder answered his question with defiant silence.

'Remember your Family Group,' cautioned the Administrator. 'Its safety depends on you.'

The Second Elder hung his head in defeat. 'It *is* the First Elder,' he confirmed. 'He says we have misjudged the people from Earth. The Doctor has gone down into the aqueduct and his companions, Susan and Ian, have gone to rescue him. . . . He is asking why I do not reply.'

The Administrator clapped his hands with joy. 'Excellent! No one can come out of there alive. The Doctor and his fellow Earth-creatures are near death. Victory for all my plans!'

The Doctor had progressed about a mile into the tunnel, following the route of the largest water pipe. Apart from the gentle grumbling of the pumping system there was no other sound; and as his torchlight played upon the tunnel walls he could see nothing out of the ordinary.

Suddenly he glimpsed a small patch of something on the ground before him. Excitedly he took a magnifying glass out of his equipment case and bent down to examine his discovery.

A look of triumph flashed across his face. He had found a small clump of plants with dull grey leaves and tiny black berries. He uprooted one and noted its long tapering roots.

'Just as I thought!' he congratulated himself. '*Atropa belladonna* – Deadly Nightshade!'

He was about to take a specimen box out of his case when he heard a terrifyingly loud growl from somewhere nearby. He stood up, ready to run, and looked this way and that in panic, unsure of where the noise was coming from.

Something else was in the tunnels with him, hiding in the shadows, waiting to spring.

The Monsters of the Caves had found him.

9

Surrounded by Enemies

The blood-curdling sound reverberated down the length of the pipe to the central chamber at the aqueduct entrance. To Ian and Susan who had just arrived there the noise sounded like a voice from deepest Hell.

'What is it, Ian?' Susan asked fearfully.

Her companion shrugged his shoulders. 'I don't know – but we must find the Doctor before it's too late!'

As if in answer a second noise came to them from down the tunnel. But this noise was shriller, more human. It was a cry of terror and pain.

'*Grandfather!*' screamed Susan. Helping Ian along she hurried down the tunnel in the direction of her grandfather's cry.

It was the longest journey of Susan's life. Even with the light of a radio-electric torch, progress down the dark winding tunnel was unbearably slow; and Ian who was still very weak from poisoning slowed her down even more. The invisible Monsters of the Caves continued their deafening roars, threatening any moment to leap out from the shadows and attack them. And all the while her grandfather might be lying injured and bleeding, perhaps even dying. It was a thought she could hardly bring herself to contemplate.

Finally after what seemed like hours but was in fact only a few minutes, they found the battered body of the Doctor. He was lying by the pipeline, his face macabrely illuminated by the light of his fallen torch. Leaving Ian to stagger on as best he could, Susan was at her grandfather's side in an instant.

She heaved a sigh of relief: the Doctor was still alive and semi-conscious. Ian came over to her and together they helped the old man to his feet. As they started to move on, anxious to escape from this dark place of unknown terror, the Doctor seemed to regain his bearings, helping considerably their progress back along the tunnel to the aqueduct entrance.

Even so, they had to pause periodically on the way to enable the injured Doctor to catch his breath. During one of these rests Susan remarked that the growls of the Monsters seemed to be more distant. Ian guessed that the animals, frightened by their presence, had retreated to their secret lair somewhere deep within the cave system. By the time they reached the bright safety of the aqueduct entrance they could no longer hear the creatures' threatening roars.

Exhausted, they collapsed near the entrance. Susan helped the Doctor off with his frock coat: it was in a very sorry state: apart from being muddied and dirty, the back of it had been slashed to ribbons.

'They don't look like claw marks,' Ian said slowly, and then examined the Doctor's back. 'Strange that whatever did that to you didn't reach your skin . . .' he remarked.

Now almost fully recovered from his shock, the Doctor added his suspicions to Ian's. 'Strange indeed when you realise I was at the mercy of that creature; it was so dark in there that it was practically invisible and it knocked me to the ground.'

'You didn't see it then?' asked Ian.

'Nonono. Something hit me under the heart: it was most unpleasant. It's a good thing that I sent you that antidote, my boy. Otherwise I might have been done for . . .'

'But we didn't get the antidote, Grandfather,' Susan interjected. 'We had to send for some more.'

The Doctor's interest was immediately aroused. 'So . . . we are surrounded by enemies: the poisoned water, those monsters in there and now, from what you say, it seems that someone among the Sensorites bears us ill will: two separate enemies . . .'

'Two?' queried Ian. 'Surely you mean three?'

'No – two,' the Doctor stated quite categorically. 'The monsters and the water are connected: I've more or less solved that little problem.' The Doctor noted with mischievous pleasure the mystified faces of his two companions and continued: 'But this Sensorite who is against us is a much greater danger. I suggest we go back and find out which one it is!'

The Doctor staggered to his feet and with Ian and Susan's

help left the central chamber.

As they did so the Sensorite Engineer moved from his hiding place behind one of the pipes. He had much to tell the City Administrator.

Unaware of Ian and Susan's success in finding and rescuing the Doctor Carol was waging a futile battle to persuade the First Elder to organise a search party of Sensorites to go to her friends' aid. Ironically, she was fighting exactly the same kind of frightened complacency which Ian had found in her and Maitland on board the spaceship.

'We just can't get up!' she said. 'You know the aqueduct: surely you can help in some way . . .'

The First Elder shook his head regretfully. 'It is impossible,' he said. 'You have no conception of what extreme sound does to us. It stuns the brain and paralyses the nerves.'

The Senior Scientist supported his leader's argument. 'In the dark we would be more of a hindrance than a help.'

Carol hung her head in defeat. The First Elder approached her in an effort to comfort her. 'You are sad for the friends you have lost,' he said softly. 'Rejoice instead for the friend who has been returned to you.' Carol looked up, expectation shining in her eyes as he continued: 'I hear that the man called John is making excellent progress – the final treatment is to begin today.'

'Thank you . . .'

'If you would like I can take you to see him,' offered the Senior Scientist.

'Yes,' said Carol gratefully. 'Yes, I would like that very much.'

To imagine John completely cured was enough to break Carol's heart: at last the nightmare of the past thirteen months would be at an end, and they could resume their normal life.

John was still attached to the mind restorer, and was only partly conscious when Carol walked into the treatment room with the Senior Scientist. The Sensorite had assured her that there was nothing to worry about: the final treatment would rebalance John's mind and return to her the man she had loved and missed for such a long time. She sat by her fiancé, stroking his hand, and listened to the words he was muttering: 'Treachery . . . a plot . . .'

Carol looked over to the Senior Scientist who was watching their display of affection with interest.

'He keeps on saying the same thing,' she said. 'Something about treachery. The Doctor told me that John might know more than we suspect. I think he's discovered something and is trying to warn us.'

'It must be a delusion,' the Senior Scientist stated with iron certainty. 'Our society is based on trust. Treason or secret plotting is impossible.'

The absurd naivety of the Senior Scientist made Carol smile involuntarily. 'That's rather a sweeping statement, isn't it?' she said.

The Sensorite was totally at a loss to understand Carol's point of view. 'Why should a Sensorite make any secret plans against anyone?' he asked. 'We have the perfect society. All are contented.'

'Some people always want more than others,' said Carol.

'That is a human value,' was the unarguable defence.

'Perhaps . . .'

Carol turned back to John who was continuing to mutter: 'Danger, I must tell you . . . but it's so difficult . . . treachery . . .'

'Don't worry, John,' Carol said softly. 'I'll be with you all the time, and soon you'll be able to tell me all you've discovered.' Concerned, she looked again to the Senior Scientist. 'Are you sure he's going to be all right?' she asked. 'He's still rambling . . .'

'He will be cured,' the Scientist assured her and then attempted to explain: 'Long ago we discovered that in our brains there are many different compartments or divisions. When fear and alarm are at work that section becomes open – a veil is lifted. This is what happened to John. But in his case the veil will not lower itself. Therefore he is constantly afraid: even when he is asleep the body says one thing and the brain another. The result: total confusion.'

'And this treatment is in order to close down this veil?' Carol tried to understand.

'Yes. Not permanently, of course. Otherwise he would step into danger without care.'

Carol searched for an analogy. 'It's rather like an eyelid,' she said and then, noticing the Scientist's confusion, explained. 'These shutters over my eyes.'

'Ah yes, of course. We Sensorites do not possess them.' There was a curious note of regret in the Scientist's voice. 'To see all the time is . . . not a good thing . . .'

After the Engineer had watched the Doctor, Ian and Susan depart he had hurried back to the Disintegrator Room. His relief at leaving the dark seclusion of the aqueduct was tempered somewhat by the panic he felt in having learnt of the Earth-creatures' suspicions and discoveries.

When he returned he found the City Administrator still revelling in the power he now enjoyed over his former superior. The Second Elder's hands were still tied firmly behind his back and he was slumped despondently in a chair.

'What are we to do?' despaired the Engineer after he had told the Administrator his news.

The evil Sensorite remained calm as he paced the room, reaffirming his beliefs to his servant. 'These Earth-creatures are working to destroy the Sensorite Nation,' he stated. 'Their pleasant smiles conceal sharp teeth; their soft words hide deadly threats. And who oppose them? Weak and timid creatures like the Second Elder here.'

He approached his former chief. 'Betrayer of our people! Coward!' He spat out the words. 'I should imprison you in some room wherein no light can shine and fill that room with noise!'

The Second Elder hung his head in hopeless resignation. 'Do it then,' he sighed. 'Finish with me . . .'

The Administrator regarded him with pleasure, deriving great satisfaction from his humiliation. 'Not yet,' he said. 'Remember your Family Group. First you shall do something for me. Summon the Senior Warrior with your mind transmitter and tell him to bring the Firing Key to the Disintegrator. He is to meet you in the forecourt of the Palace of the Elders.'

'No. I cannot do such a thing,' he protested, recalling the

Administrator's original plans for the humans. 'The humans are not as you see them. They are good people.'

'Remember your Family Group!'

Reluctantly the Second Elder nodded his head in agreement. At a sign from the Administrator the Engineer untied the prisoner's hands. The Second Elder took his mind transmitter from the Administrator and put it to his forehead. As he sent out his message his captor listened in to the mental conversation.

When the message had been sent the Administrator snatched the mind transmitter from him. 'Excellent!' he cried. '*I* shall keep the appointment you have made. The Senior Warrior shall know me by the sash I wear. Once I have the Firing Key I shall put down the threat of the Earth-creatures forever.' He marched triumphantly out of the room.

The Elder looked on as he left. 'Why do you listen to him?' he asked the Engineer.

The Engineer regarded the Second Elder with scorn. '*He* will not betray our people nor surrender our planet,' he claimed. 'He will be the saviour of the Sensorite Nation.'

The Second Elder shook his head from side to side in despair. How could he make the Engineer see the truth of the matter? How could he make him realise the consequences of the Administrator's mad acts? 'Don't you understand?' he pleaded. 'He will bring us all down!'

Such was the Sensorites' deference to authority that the Senior Warrior had hastened with all speed to the Palace forecourt when he had received the Second Elder's telepathic message. He had not even questioned the Second Elder's motive for wanting the Firing Key. And so it was only a matter of minutes before the Administrator, wearing the Second Elder's sash, once more had the Firing Key in his possession.

As he dismissed the Warrior and was about to return to the Disintegrator Room, he spotted the Doctor, Ian and Susan. They had returned from the aqueduct and were just now entering the Palace forecourt.

'Isn't that one of the Elders?' asked the Doctor.

'It's the Second Elder,' confirmed Susan. 'You can tell by

the single sash he's wearing.'

'I'd like a word with him,' said the Doctor and promptly followed the Sensorite who, upon seeing the Doctor's party, had begun to leave the forecourt hurriedly.

'I say! You, sir!' cried the Doctor and set off in pursuit.

Susan smiled at her grandfather's new vitality. 'It's a funny place down here isn't it?' she remarked to Ian.

'What about up there?' said Ian, raising his eyes heavenwards. 'I wonder how Barbara's doing on the spaceship?'

'I wish she was down here with us,' sighed the girl.

'Why don't we ask the First Elder if she can come down and join us now?' wondered Ian.

Susan nodded eagerly and then greeted her grandfather who had given up his chase of the 'Second Elder'. His face was flushed.

'Most extraordinary!' he panted. 'He ran away from me!'

Susan began to giggle. 'That must have looked funny, what with those silly round feet! Flip-flop! Flip-flop!'

The Doctor and Ian joined in her merriment. 'I can assure you, he was extremely mobile!' laughed the Doctor. 'Now, come on, let's go and see the First Elder.'

Breathless from his sudden burst of unaccustomed physical activity the Administrator stumbled into the Disintegrator Room and triumphantly displayed the Firing Key to his subordinate. 'Now I have the power!' he exclaimed. 'Soon the Earth-creatures will be no more!'

Suddenly everything seemed to happen at once. The Engineer had neglected to retie the Second Elder's hands after they had been released in order to use the mind transmitter. With a mighty bound the Second Elder leapt out of his chair and pushed the Engineer aside.

In one swift action he wrenched the Firing Key from the Administrator's hand and began to bash it down violently on the side of the Disintegrator console.

The Administrator tried furiously to stop him and called on the Engineer to help him. Staggering to his feet the Engineer seized a heavy metal bar from a nearby workbench. Without thinking what he was doing he struck the Second Elder a crushing blow on the head. The Second Elder let out a pained cry and fell to the ground.

The Administrator looked angrily down at the Firing Key which was now totally useless. 'He has destroyed it!' he exploded. 'The only other Firing Key is in the possession of the First Elder and he will not part with it to anyone!'

But the Engineer was not listening. He stood staring, unbelieving, at the motionless body of the Second Elder on the floor. 'He is dead,' he whispered.

Then panic took control of him. 'We must leave the City at once,' he urged. 'We must hide in the mountains!'

For a moment the Administrator also stood still, shocked by the enormity of the crime: *a Sensorite killed by a fellow Sensorite*. Then he recovered possession of himself: yet another plan was forming in his sly and opportunistic mind. He could use this undoubted tragedy to his own advantage.

'No, do not be foolish,' he said to his nervous associate. 'The death of the Second Elder can *help* us, not condemn us. We must act quickly. I will outline my plan to you . . .'

A Conspiracy of Lies

Ever since Ian's outburst the First Elder had been examining his attitude towards the strangers and had found it lacking in compassion and sympathy, two qualities the Sensorites prized in themselves. During the anxious hours while Ian and Susan had been searching for the old man he had been tormented by a totally alien feeling: guilt. He had merely sought to use the humans to find an antidote for the atropine poisoning, never realising that they too had feelings. Ian had made him acknowledge the great debt he owed them; indeed, the schoolteacher's willingness to risk his life for his friend was worthy of any Sensorite.

So it was with enormous relief that he greeted the Doctor's safe return, and he had instantly seen that all his needs were catered for; he had also thought of Carol and sent a messenger to the Medical Unit to give her the happy news.

Now the Doctor, Ian and Susan were once again seated in the First Elder's chamber, gratefully sipping at the crystal water and discussing the peculiar sequence of events which had resulted in Ian's not being given the antidote to the atropine poisoning.

'I have made enquiries,' the First Elder told them. 'The first supply of the antidote was apparently interrupted by my Second Elder, and he has since disappeared.'

'We saw him in the courtyard,' Susan informed him. 'Grandfather wanted to talk to him and he ran away.

'You just won't accept that he's done something wrong, will you?' Ian persisted.

'I cannot: it is inconceivable that he should do such a thing.' Despite his firm words the First Elder seemed distressed and confused by his deputy's strange behaviour. 'I selected him for office . . . I know that Sensorite and trust him implicitly.'

'And yet you can't explain his actions,' Susan pointed out

with hard simplicity.

The First Elder silenced her. 'A mystery does not mean he is guilty. There will be valid reasons for his actions.' Somehow his voice lacked conviction; the humans' questions had raised doubts in his mind, doubts which if proved, could completely shatter the mutual trust which was the base of order in the Sensorite City.

A Sensorite servant entered the room, interrupting the conversation. Bowing low to his leader he presented him with a long black cloak. 'For the Doctor,' he explained.

The Doctor stood up and graciously accepted the cloak. It really was a most splendid garment, made of heavy black velvet and lined with red silk; as he tried it on he realised just what a dashing figure he cut in it.

'*Very* smart,' Susan said admiringly.

'Beau Brummel always used to say I looked better in a cloak,' the Doctor reminded her before thanking the First Elder and his servant. 'This is really most civil of you! I ruined my jacket down in the aqueduct.'

The First Elder politely acknowledged the Doctor's thanks and dismissed his servant. As he left the room he was passed by the City Administrator. He had now taken off the sash of Second Elder and was wearing his own collar of office.

'The City Administrator wishes to speak?' queried the First Elder, slightly irritated by this further interruption.

'Urgently, sir. I have something you should hear.' The Administrator's tone was solicitous. 'It concerns the Second Elder.'

'Very well, speak.' This Sensorite was tiresome and irritating at the best of times, thought the First Elder; but it could be in their interests to hear what he had to say.

With the First Elder's permission the Administrator called the Senior Warrior and the Sensorite Engineer into the room.

The Engineer approached the First Elder, pointedly ignoring the party of humans. 'Sir, the Second Elder is dead: he was killed in the courtyard,' he said slowly.

The First Elder looked to the Administrator who nodded his head. 'What he says is true, sir,' he confirmed. 'The Engineer has shown me his body.'

'I saw the man who killed him,' continued the Engineer.

102

'*Man?*'

'Yes. It was the man called the Doctor,' he declared.

Susan rose instantly to her feet in defence of her grandfather. 'But that's not true!' she claimed fervently. The Doctor put a restraining hand on her arm, urging her to be calm.

The Administrator ignored her outburst and beckoned the Senior Warrior forward. The First Elder gave him leave to speak.

'I met the Second Elder in the courtyard as he ordered me to,' the Warrior said, believing that he was speaking the truth. 'I gave him the Firing Key to the Disintegrator. Then I saw the Doctor go after the Second Elder.'

'That is perfectly true, sir.' The Doctor's voice was steady, but there was a challenge in his eyes. 'I wished to speak to him – but I did not kill him.'

The Engineer embroidered his lie. 'I saw the Doctor wrestle for possession of the Firing Key,' he claimed.

'And here it is – bent as if in a struggle.' The Administrator produced the broken Firing Key from beneath his tunic.

'And when the Second Elder refused to give up the Key I saw the Doctor take an object from his coat and knock the Second Elder down to the ground and kill him.' The Engineer completed his deception, satisfied that he had played his role to perfection.

The First Elder walked slowly up to the Doctor's party. They were now all sitting in stunned silence.

'This is a grave accusation,' he said sternly.

'And obviously untrue,' sir,' declared Ian, standing up and moving over to the Engineer. Some time ago on a distant planet the Doctor had proved Ian's innocence in a murder trial. Now it was time to return the favour.

He faced the Engineer squarely in the face. 'How did you recognise the Doctor?' he asked.

The Engineer hesitated a moment before replying. 'His hair is different.'

'And?' Ian clearly wasn't satisfied with the answer.

Confused, the Engineer stumbled on. 'So are his clothes.' By his side the Administrator was equally puzzled by Ian's apparently purposeless questioning but he was in no position to warn his accomplice to be on his guard.

'Oh yes, his clothes,' Ian seized on the answer. Behind him the Doctor and Susan exchanged a mutual look of understanding. 'You say that you saw him take an object from his pocket. You could see quite clearly?'

The Engineer nodded. What in the stars was this devious Earth-creature getting at?

Ian continued: 'You are sure it was from his *coat* pocket?'

'Yes. I have already said that.' The Engineer was becoming even more confused. 'Every Sensorite knows the Doctor by –'

He stopped. All eyes were on the Doctor who had risen to his feet and was preening himself magnificently in his new cloak.

'The Doctor's coat was left behind in the aqueduct,' Ian finished his defence. 'You were lying.'

'Then . . . then it was a cloak he was wearing,' claimed the Engineer, panicking now. 'Yes, I'm sure of that now.'

It was now the First Elder's turn to speak. 'I have just given the Doctor that cloak.' He regarded the Engineer with distaste. 'Your story is a tissue of lies. Senior Warrior – remove this Sensorite!'

As the Warrior escorted the Engineer away, the Administrator waddled solicitously up to the First Elder. He was concerned lest he be thought involved in any way in the Engineer's deception.

'Sir, you must forgive his wild accusations,' he whined. 'I did what I thought was right. I felt his story should be heard.'

'You acted correctly,' he reassured him. There was sadness and disappointment in his voice. 'By his lies the Engineer has proved his guilt. But what could have affected the Second Elder so much that he should want the Firing Key to the Disintegrator?'

'The Second Elder was always opposed to our visitors,' said the Administrator cunningly. 'He took the Firing Key to attack them with the power of the Distintegrator.'

'I bet he took the antidote too!' piped up Susan, unknowingly giving support to the evil Sensorite's lies. 'He was our enemy all along!'

The First Elder signalled an end to the discussion. 'This is a sad matter . . . but since the Second Elder too has betrayed us my sympathy shall not be wasted on him. We must now turn our minds to choosing his successor.'

The Administrator produced the Second Elder's sash from beneath his tunic. 'I have his sash of office here,' he said, handing it to his leader.

The Doctor's party had been watching the scene between the two Sensorites with interest. Suddenly Ian had an idea.

'Perhaps the First Elder doesn't need to look further than this room for the Second Elder's replacement,' he suggested to his friends.

Susan warmed to the notion. 'Of course! If the Administrator gets high office because of us he'd make a valuable ally.'

'Precisely what I was thinking!' beamed the Doctor. Effecting his most statesmanlike manner he strode up to the First Elder.

'We have no wish to interfere in your affairs,' he began diplomatically, 'but the City Administrator seems to have all the qualities of a Second Elder. Perhaps he might be the ideal choice for your advisor?'

The First Elder considered the matter. True, the City Administrator could be annoying and at times too eager to please, but he had always served the Sensorite Nation faithfully, running the City on smooth and efficient lines. All he did was for the greater good of the Sensorites. And if he could instill such confidence in these humans . . .

'Can you accept and use justly supreme power and supreme authority?' he asked the Administrator who was positively quivering with excited anticipation.

The Administrator chose his words deliberately. 'My only ambition is to serve the Sensorite Nation,' he claimed.

The First Elder silently congratulated himself: it was the right answer – the role of Second Elder was not for those who harboured personal ambition.

With due ceremony he removed the Administrator's collar and replaced it with the sash of Second Elder. 'Accept this sash. I make you my advisor,' he pronounced. 'From this moment on you will be known as Second Elder, second on the Sense-Sphere only to me. And once this order has been made only a breach of trust can set it aside.'

The Administrator raised his bowed head with genuine pride, and smiled a secret smile. At last the Sensorite Nation would have as one of its leaders a Sensorite of courage and vision, one who would lead the Sensorites on to greatness; and to think that these stupid Earth-creatures had played right into his hands and brought him to this position! It only confirmed what he already knew: they were obviously inferior beings.

After performing the investiture the First Elder requested that the Doctor, Ian and Susan leave him and his new advisor to discuss matters arising from the new appointment.

'Certainly, sir,' agreed the Doctor. 'My companions and I will pay a visit to John and note his progress.'

As the Doctor led his friends out of the room Susan reminded Ian about asking permission for Barbara to come down to the planet. 'This isn't quite the time,' he remarked wryly, smiling at the puffed-up figure of the Administrator. He was revelling in his new office as Second Elder. As they made to leave, Ian offered his congratulations to the Sensorite.

The Administrator looked at the Earthman with obvious disdain and snapped back, 'When you address one of the Elders you call him sir!'

For two long days John had been submitted to treatment on the Sensorites' mind restorer and now was the moment of truth. Carol watched on nervously as the Senior Scientist unstrapped John from the chair, removing the domed apparatus from his head and disconnecting the wires which had been taped to his body. Within minutes she would know whether the man she had loved would ever be cured and returned to her. Her whole future hinged on the outcome.

John groaned and raised his hands to his eyes, rubbing them in an attempt to refocus his vision. Carol bent down to him, looking enquiringly in his face for any sign of recognition.

'Carol . . . my head . . . hurts . . .' he complained.

'That will pass,' the Senior Scientist assured him and distanced himself slightly from the couple.

John smiled down affectionately at his fiancée and stroked

a lock of her hair. His voice was soft and tender, all fear finally taken away. 'Carol, he said, you're crying.'

'I'm all right, John, really I am,' she sobbed. 'It's just that I haven't seen you smile in such a long time . . .'

'But we can't have you crying, can we?' he chided her good-naturedly. 'I'm better now – there's no need to worry anymore.'

'All those months with you, scared, frightened, never knowing who I was – it was so awful. Do you remember any of it at all?'

John shuddered involuntarily, thinking back to his time on board the spaceship. 'Some of it,' he said, 'but most of the time it seems like a bad dream, a nightmare.' He smiled at Carol again. 'All I really know is that it seem a very long time.'

He stood up from the chair and Carol rose to take him lovingly in her arms. 'Oh, John, I can't tell you how I feel,' she whispered. She kissed him, running her fingers through his hair which was now completely black, visible proof of the success of the Sensorites' treatment. 'Welcome home, John, welcome home.'

The Senior Scientist had been observing this display of love with curiosity: such ostentation was unknown to the highly sophisticated Sensorite race. 'It is indeed a time of great happiness for both of you,' he ventured.

Carol smiled her agreement and introduced the Scientist to John as the one who had cured him. John held out his hand to the Scientist.

'What do you ask for?' asked the puzzled Sensorite.

John smiled. 'We have a custom on Earth of shaking hands with someone in friendship,' he said.

The Senior Scientist reflected for a moment on the humans' peculiar predilection for physical contact, and then offered his hand in return. 'Then I accept your friendship,' he said, 'as I hope you will accept mine.'

It was at this happy scene that the Doctor, Ian and Susan entered the room. Susan bounced up to John, glad to see that he was completely recovered from his traumatic ordeal. 'Do you remember us?' she chirped.

John grinned. 'I remember *you* distinctly,' he teased.

Ian laughed as Susan flushed with embarrassment. 'Well, I'm Ian,' he said, 'and this is the Doctor, Susan's grand-father. Barbara, our other companion, is up in the spaceship with Captain Maitland.'

The Doctor stepped forward. 'I'm glad to see that you don't bear any grudges towards the Sensorites, young man,' he said.

'That's all in the past now, Doctor. We've got to think about the present – and the future.' He winked at Carol, who tightened her grip on his hand.

'Excellent, excellent,' approved the Doctor. Perhaps there was hope for Ian and Barbara's preposterous species after all if such good sense prevailed into the twenty-eighth century. He turned to the Senior Scientist and indicated that he should accompany him: he wanted to check on the progress of the manufacture and distribution of the antidote to the atropine poisoning.

As the two scientists left the room they failed to notice the Administrator who quickly concealed himself in an archway in the passage outside. When the Doctor and his Sensorite associate had passed, he returned to the half-open door of the Medical Unit and listened.

'John,' began Susan, 'all the time you were ill you were trying to tell us something.'

John tried to recreate those painful memories. 'Yes . . there was a Sensorite here who was dangerous. It's all very hazy, but I know there was a plot against you.'

All eyes turned as the Administrator abruptly entered the room. 'Can you identify this Sensorite?' he asked cautiously.

John shook his head. 'No . . . but I do remember there was something peculiar about his clothes. I remember – '

The Sensorite cut him short. 'Yes. It must have been the Sensorite who has just been killed,' he said hastily and then turned to Susan. 'The First Elder wishes to talk to the Doctor. You will inform him,' he said crisply and walked smartly out of the room.

'All right!' she said, indignant at his curtness. She pulled a face at his back as the door closed behind him.

'He's not very friendly,' remarked Ian.

'He's just been made Second Elder, remember,' said Susan.

108

'I imagine he's trying out his new authority.'

'Well, I wouldn't like to cross him!' laughed Carol. 'Come on, let's go and find the Doctor.

The production of the antidote was progressing at a steady rate and with typical Sensorite efficiency. Reports of successful treatments were coming in from all parts of the City. In the Scientific Unit itself the Doctor was welcomed with great respect and some awe: it was a state of affairs he thoroughly approved of.

Satisfied that all his instructions were being followed the Doctor turned his attention to rummaging through the files and records of the Scientific Unit – all in the name of research, of course. As the Doctor had reminded Ian some time ago he could never be accused of being overly curious . . .

When Ian and the others found him, he and the Senior Scientist were poring over a mass of papers and objects. Among them was a large map.

'What's all that?' asked Ian.

The Doctor looked up. 'Things left behind by the humans in the spacecraft that exploded,' he explained. 'Family snapshots, mementoes, that sort of thing. But this here is very interesting.' He showed Ian the map. 'It's a rough plan of the aqueduct.'

'Yes, one of the humans was very interested in the aqueduct,' added the Senior Scientist.

'Is that so?' asked the Doctor with real interest.

Susan suddenly remembered the reason they had come in search of the Doctor. 'Grandfather, the First Elder wants to talk to you.'

The Doctor grunted with indifference, far more concerned with the map. Noticing his interest, the Senior Scientist offered to provide him with a proper plan of the aqueduct system, rather than the rough sketch he had here. 'The City Administrator can surely have no objection,' he said and left the room.

Ever since her last meeting with the Administrator, there had been something nagging at the back of Susan's mind. Perhaps it was just intuition, or this special sixth sense she seemed to possess on the Sense-Sphere, but something had seemed not quite right. Suddenly she realised what it was. 'The City Administrator!' she cried. 'It was him!'

'What on Earth are you talking about, child?' asked the Doctor.

'The Sensorite who was against us: the Administrator said it was the Second Elder, the Sensorite who had just died. But the Administrator was wearing the Second Elder's sash . . .' she said excitedly.

'What are you getting at Susan?' asked Ian, as mystified as the Doctor.

'Don't you see?' the girl went on, stamping her foot in frustration. 'We can only tell the difference between the Sensorites by the sashes they wear. If the Second Elder really was the culprit, why didn't John recognise the Administrator as our enemy – he was wearing the Second Elder's sash.' She looked at John. 'John, you said there was something odd about the evil Sensorite. Was it his collar?'

'Yes, that was it!' John confirmed.

'Then the City Administrator is our enemy,' declared Susan triumphantly.

Ian let Susan's arguments sink in. 'The one who's just been made Second Elder . . .'

'Yes.' Susan nodded enthusiastically. 'When John was ill he must have given himself away.'

'If this is true, Susan, we are in serious trouble,' said the Doctor. 'That Sensorite has power now.'

'Yes,' agreed Ian. 'And what is worse, we gave it to him . . .'

The Doctor and Ian had learned enough of Sensorite society to realise that no accusation against the Administrator would bear weight with the First Elder unless they could back it up with hard evidence. And the only evidence they had was John's testimony, hardly enough on which to base a case.

Faced with an unfounded accusation against his chief advisor, and that advisor's claim that the humans were working against the glorious Sensorite Nation, it was easy to see who the First Elder would most readily believe. Looked at quite dispassionately, the TARDIS crew and their friends had more to gain in undermining the Sensorites: the precious molybdenum for one thing. And it was futile to ask the First Elder for that sort of trust which the Sensorites seemed to give blindly to each other.

The only way to prove their innocence and the Administrator's guilt was to go back down into the aqueduct and discover who or what was deliberately poisoning the Sensorites' water supply. Otherwise it would only be a matter of time before the wily Administrator convinced the First Elder and the Sensorites that they were responsible for bringing death to the Sense-Sphere.

After they had outlined their intention to go down to the aqueduct to the First Elder, of course omitting to tell him the real reasons for doing so, the leader of the Sensorite Nation expressed his disbelief. Surely they did not want to go back down into the noise and the darkness to face the Monsters of the Caves once more?

'I assure you, my good sir, we shall be perfectly all right,' the Doctor said confidently.

The First Elder considered. 'Very well,' he at last agreed. 'But I insist that you take light with you, and such arms as we can provide.'

As the Doctor and Ian agreed the Elder raised his mind transmitter to his forehead to contact his Senior Warrior.

(In another part of the Palace the Senior Warrior acknowledged his leader's command and made his way to the Armoury.)

'Now, we do have a little problem, sir: my granddaughter Susan,' began the Doctor.

The First Elder tilted his head in interest as the Doctor continued: 'She's sure to want to come with us; and between you and me, she might get in the way, I wonder if you would mind keeping a little secret for me?'

'It shall be done,' the First Elder conceded. 'I shall not let her know of your trip to the aqueduct.'

Ian breathed a sigh of relief and gratitude. Despite what the Doctor had said to the First Elder their expedition might indeed prove to be dangerous, and the less Susan knew about it the better. Recently she had been showing a marked independence of spirit and if she found out about the journey she would have insisted on accompanying them. And the dark cave system was certainly not the place for a young girl.

'I wonder too, sir,' said the Doctor, now somewhat pushing his luck, 'if our companion, Barbara, might be allowed to come down to the Sense-Sphere. She could keep Susan company while Chesterton and I are away . . .' The Doctor tried to study his host's enigmatic face, anxiously awaiting the answer.

'Very well,' the First Elder said resignedly. 'It will be arranged.'

'Splendid!' beamed the Doctor, once more satisfied that he had got all his own way.

It was simplicity itself for the Administrator to release the Engineer from prison. Using his newly acquired authority – this time legitimately – as Second Elder of the Sensorite Nation he had merely to request the Engineer's release from the Sensorite gaoler and it was done. No forms to fill in, no questions asked, no fuss at all: on such lines was Sensorite society run.

Back in the Disintegrator Room the Administrator received his accomplice's gushing thanks with indifference. 'You were not to know that the Doctor had changed his clothes,' he graciously allowed. 'But I still have a task for you . . .'

'Ask and it shall be done.'

The Administrator opened a small metal box which was lying on the table before him. Inside it were two hand guns. 'I have learnt that the Doctor and one of his companions are to go back down into the aqueduct,' he said. 'You are accomplished in mechanical matters. Remove the mechanisms from these guns but leave them looking perfect from the outside.'

'At once.' The Engineer picked up the guns and turned to go but the Administrator called him back.

'One more thing,' he said. From out of his tunic he drew a rolled-up map. 'This is a plan of the aqueduct. I intercepted the messenger who was to take it to the Doctor on the Senior Scientist's orders. I have altered some of the routes on it. Ensure that it is delivered to the Doctor.'

'Immediately, sir.' The Engineer took the map and left the

room, excited at his responsibilities and eager to please.

The Administrator smiled. Soon he would be rid of the Doctor and Ian Chesterton. Not only would they go down into the aqueduct with useless weapons, but they would be hopelessly lost, at the mercy of the Monsters of the Caves!

Once again the unwitting pawn of the Administrator's schemes, the Senior Warrior entered the First Elder's chamber carrying the two hand guns with which the Engineer had tampered. Upon the First Elder's command he instructed the two time-travellers in their operation.

'They are very simple to use,' he explained. 'The range is considerable and the ray can paralyse up to a distance of ninety metres.' Proud of the achievement of Sensorite technology he looked for some sign of appreciation from the Doctor and Ian.

He did not know the Doctor very well. While Ian at least affected a polite interest in the weapons, the old man casually picked up the two guns and tossed one over to Ian. 'I've never liked weapons at the best of times,' he admitted. 'But they're handy little things, I suppose.'

The Senior Warrior was crestfallen. This was most certainly not the way to talk about one of the crowning glories of Sensorite science!

'Now, how long does this paralysis last?' asked the Doctor.

'One hour' was the reply. Was it the Doctor's imagination or was the Senior Warrior really sulking?

'Well, these weapons are splendid, sir, and without a doubt they'll make our mission a great success,' he said, considerably cheering up the Senior Warrior with this praise.

'And yet I do not envy you your task,' said the First Elder.

'Oh, there's no real danger, especially not now we have these weapons,' said the Doctor. 'Our little business will be finished in an hour or so.'

A messenger entered carrying the rolled-up map which the Administrator had secretly altered. 'Splendid!' exclaimed the Doctor. 'Now, let's be on our way. Are you sure that you're up to it, Chesterton?'

Ian smiled at the old man who was as infuriatingly indefatigable as ever. 'Yes, I'm fine now, Doctor.'

The Doctor and Ian bowed to the First Elder and left the chamber. After they had left, the Sensorite messenger made so bold as to speak to his leader.

'They are very brave people, sir,' he remarked.

The First Elder agreed. 'We will not see their like again.'

'I am glad that they were innocent of the death of the Second Elder,' the messenger said.

'I am still anxious about that,' confessed the Sensorite leader. 'You realise that if they didn't kill my advisor then he must have been killed by a Sensorite . . .'

The messenger was shocked. Such a thing was unthinkable. 'But who would do such a deed?' he asked.

'Who indeed . . .' The First Elder's voice was strained. 'But I also ask myself why . . .'

Susan stared in stunned admiration at the feast the Sensorites had prepared for them in a lounge in the grounds of the Palace. Golden and silver platters were piled high with foods of every colour and description: juicy mouth-watering fruits, succulent cuts of piping hot meats, tangy cheeses and seeded breads, and goblets of the Sensorites' crystal water. This was undoubtedly the best way to end any adventure.

John and Carol laughed fondly at Susan's child-like fascination.

'I can't wait, I'm so hungry,' she said, licking her lips. 'But where on Earth have Grandfather and Ian got to?'

'I expect they're finalising our return to the spaceship,' Carol said. 'I think I'll go to the Palace and hurry them up.'

'Tell them I'm starving too!' John called after her as she left the room.

'John,' Susan said when they were alone, 'I'm so glad you're better now. So's Carol – well, you can see that for yourself,' she said, stating the obvious.

'She's had a bad time of it all,' John sighed. 'I've a feeling we'll both give up space travel when we get back to Earth.'

'And get married?' asked Susan.

'Yes. She's all I really care about.'

There was an awkward silence. Happy to be a witness to a real-life love story, Susan still felt a pang of jealousy. Carol and John would soon be going home, settling down, raising a family . . . She had been travelling so long with her grandfather that she no longer had a real home: even at Coal Hill School she had always been the odd one out.

She loved being with the Doctor and could never leave him; but sometimes she longed for an end to the ceaseless wanderings through time and space, and pined for the companionship of someone her own age.

'Cheer up, Susan,' said John, interrupting her melancholy. 'Come on, let's eat. I'm tired of waiting.'

He handed her a large orange which she gratefully accepted.

It was the happiest time of Carol's life. John was well, soon they would be reunited with Maitland and Barbara, and then they would be on their way home to start a new life together. She dreamt of the happy times they would share: weekends spent miles away from Central City in the countryside; candlelit evenings for two; starting a family.

If Carol had not been so wrapped up in these happy thoughts, she might have heard the soft footfall of the Engineer creeping up behind her as she made her way to the Palace. A wad of cloth soaked in a sickly smelling chemical was suddenly pressed against her mouth. Everything went black and Carol slipped to the floor, unconscious.

11

The Secret of the Caves

Carol came to in the Disintegrator Room. Hovering scornfully about her were the City Administrator and his accomplice. Their very bearing towards her radiated their hate and contempt.

'Why are you doing this to me?' she demanded groggily.

The Administrator threw a notepad and pen down onto the table beside her. 'Pay careful attention to me,' he snapped. 'You will write a letter to the man John.'

'I will not!' she retorted.

'To argue is a waste of time,' the Administrator stated coldly. 'Two of your friends are up in the spaceship; two have gone down to the aqueduct; and the man John and the girl Susan are waiting innocently for you in the Rest Area. Your party is divided – and you are helpless.'

The Administrator's plain statement of the facts forced Carol to realise the hopelessness of her situation and the futility of resistance. 'What do you want me to do?' she asked submissively.

'Tell him that you have returned to the spaceship,' he ordered. 'Then he will not suspect your disappearance.'

'You can't force me to do that,' she protested feebly.

'I can see that you stay alive,' the Administrator argued deriving almost sadistic pleasure from Carol's helplessness. 'Your life means nothing to me: so let us strike a bargain. You will write the note and I shall see that you live.'

Carol hung her head in defeat, succumbing to the Administrator's cruel arguments. Meekly she gave her consent and reached for the pen and began to write. The Administrator looked on gloatingly.

After she had finished he took up the paper, passed a cursory glance over it and then turned to his fellow Sensorite.

'You will stay here and guard her while I arrange for the message to be delivered,' he commanded. 'She will directly lead to the success of all my plans.'

'And I shall be given high office?' the Engineer asked.

'I shall reward all those who are faithful to me,' the Administrator promised.

As he left the room, Carol slumped into her chair by the Disintegrator console. Just when everything seemed to be going so well and they were about to return home the world had come crashing down about her. A hundred wild thoughts and questions passed through her mind. What would happen to her now? Surely the Administrator would not allow her to survive? Or would she be used as a lure to bring John and Susan down to this room where they too would be killed?

From the corner of the room the Engineer watched her closely, relishing the sight of an Earth-creature finally brought down to its proper place.

Concerned that Carol had not returned after an hour, John and Susan had gone off to the Palace in search of her. As they crossed the courtyard a Sensorite messenger hurriedly pressed a note into Susan's hand and then rushed off.

John took the paper from Susan and unfolded it. *'John – have gone up to the spaceship – Carol,'* he read. He showed the note to Susan. 'I don't understand,' he said. 'Why should she suddenly leave without telling us?'

'I don't know,' admitted Susan, 'but there's something peculiar about all this – I can feel it. Let's talk to the First Elder.'

The two were shown into the First Elder's chamber with the courtesy which was now customary and were asked to wait.

To their great surprise and delight Barbara was also there awaiting an audience with the Sensorite leader. The First Elder had wasted no time in complying with the Doctor's request and he had sent a Sensorite up to the spaceship to bring the teacher down to the Sense-Sphere. After Susan had reintroduced Barbara to John, she quickly recounted their adventures on the Sense-Sphere and showed her Carol's note.

'She wouldn't have gone up to the spaceship without telling us,' Susan insisted.

John added his voice to Susan's. 'If she had done, Barbara would have seen her or at least passed her on the way,' he said.

Barbara agreed. 'She was obviously forced to write this. But whoever did it didn't know that I was being brought down to the planet.'

'I bet the City Administrator had something to do with it!' Susan accused.

'But why kidnap her?' John wanted to know.

'I should think that's obvious, don't you?' said Barbara.

'No, I don't. We're all on very good terms with the First Elder now that the Doctor's discovered an antidote for the poison,' he said.

'Look – I've been up in the spaceship so perhaps I can see things more clearly,' Barbara explained patiently. 'I think we're being used by one of the Sensorites in an attempt to seize power. Sooner or later I'm sure we'll have a ransom note. Or Carol will somehow be used to discredit us and to prove that we are responsible for the poisoning of the Sensorites' water.'

'You mean we're not just being attacked because we're from another planet?' asked Susan.

Barbara shook her head. 'No . . . though I'd be surprised if that didn't have something to do with it,' she said, and then looked up as the First Elder entered the room.

'I welcome you,' he said cordially. 'Your friends expressed so much concern about you that I arranged for you to be brought down to the Sense-Sphere.'

Barbara smiled at her host's studied good manners. 'Thank you,' she said, 'but I'm afraid we must ask for yet another favour. The Doctor and Ian are missing. Do you have any idea where they might be?' She noticed the First Elder's hesitation and pressed further. 'Please tell me.'

The Elder tactfully avoided a direct answer. 'There is a quality in human beings which intrigues me,' he said, deftly changing the subject, 'and that is your concern for each other. I can assure you that your two friends are safe . . .'

'You *do* know where they are, then?' Barbara persisted.

'Yes – but they asked me not to tell you where they went,' Susan sighed with irritation. 'That's Grandfather!' she complained.

Seeing that she would get no further information from the Sensorite about the Doctor and Ian's whereabouts, Barbara handed him Carol's note. She asked him to read it.

'I gave no such order,' he said after a while.

'We didn't think you did,' Barbara remarked.

'Then why did your friend write what is not true? It *is* her writing, I presume?' Not for the first time the First Elder was deeply puzzled by the humans' questions and actions.

'Because someone made her write it!' cried John, infuriated by the Sensorite's unbelievable naivety.

'She could not have travelled without my orders,' the First Elder said with assurance. 'Where did you receive this?'

'In the courtyard near the archways,' answered Susan.

'She is being held prisoner,' John said, finding it increasingly difficult to keep his temper in the face of the First Elder's absurd calm.

'Not by any Sensorite,' the First Elder told him.

'*Of course she is!*' burst out John. Barbara urged him to lower his voice as the First Elder stepped back in pain.

Susan indicated a smudge of ink on the letter. 'Look – when this was given to me the ink wasn't quite dry. I put my finger on it and smudged it. That smudge means it must have been written just before we got it.'

'Are you implying that your friend Carol is being held prisoner in this Palace?' The First Elder made it clear that such a thing was impossible without his knowledge.

Once again that insufferable self-assurance. Barbara bit her lip in an effort to remain calm. 'Are there any other buildings in this vicinity?' she asked.

'Only the Disintegrator Room,' answered the Sensorite.

'Where's that?'

'Below the courtyard. It is rarely used now.'

'Then that must be where they're holding Carol prisoner!' cried John. 'We must rescue her.'

'I cannot unravel this mystery but I see that it worries you. I shall entrust to you the services of my Senior Warrior.' The First Elder paused for a moment, regarding the humans thoughtfully; and then he said, 'As for your other friends I must tell you that they have gone down into the aqueduct.'

'*What!*'

The First Elder urged Susan to remain calm. 'They were given light and a good map. They were also well armed. Rest easy: they are in no danger whatsoever.'

Down in the aqueduct Ian threw the two hand guns to the ground. 'The inside filaments have been removed, Doctor,' he said. 'The weapons are absolutely useless.'

'That's only one of our problems, dear boy,' said the Doctor sadly. He directed the feeble light of his torch onto the unfurled map before him. 'This map is of no use to us either. Look – all the lines and routes have been altered; someone's been jigging about with it.'

Ian made an attempt at optimism. 'We'll still get out of here somehow, Doctor.' He hoped he sounded confident.

'Oh yes – in time,' agreed his companion. 'But do we have that time? We brought no food with us and the only water we have here is that poisoned water. And to top it all we don't know what else is down here with us. What a charming outlook!'

As if in answer to his complaint, from down one of the side tunnels there came a low rumbling, like the growl of an awakening wild beast. The Doctor quickly got to his feet and with Ian began to try and find a way out of the tunnel system – before whatever horror that dwelt in the aqueduct found them.

Carol looked up in despair at the leering face of the Engineer. His obvious satisfaction at her suffering was hideous to behold.

'How long are you going to keep me here?' she asked.

'I am not permitted to say,' he said loftily.

She pleaded with him. 'Look, I've had nothing to eat and I'm very thirsty!'

'That is of no consequence.'

'But I wrote the letter!' she protested.

The Engineer looked at her with scorn. 'Surely you do not seriously believe that you are to be released?'

Carol's face fell as the meaning of the Engineer's words sank in.

'All Earth-creatures are naive,' he continued. 'They live

while they have a purpose. As soon as that purpose is achieved they have no value left.'

As the Engineer continued his tirade against his despised enemies, the door to the Disintegrator Room was suddenly smashed open. Standing in the doorway was John, his eyes wild with anger. Behind him was the Senior Warrior; he was holding aloft his hand gun. With surprising speed the Engineer grabbed a live power lead from the Disintegrator control console and waved it menacingly in Carol's face.

'Stop!' he spat at John. 'I have only to touch her with this and she will die horribly!' he threatened.

'Don't be a fool,' said John. 'Put it down. It's the end for you now.'

'No Sensorite should ever be humbled before an Earth-creature,' the Engineer declaimed hatefully.

Keeping her eye fixed on the Engineer Carol had edged her foot to the other end of the power lead. With one quick jerk she disconnected the lead from the console.

In the ensuing explosion of sparks and smoke John seized his chance and lunged for the Engineer, knocking him down to the floor. In a hand to hand struggle the small Sensorite was no match for the powerful human. John dragged him violently to his feet and flung him into the Senior Warrior's arms.

'I have already imprisoned you once,' the Warrior hissed. 'This time you will not escape.'

Covering the evil Sensorite with his hand gun he led him out of the Disintegrator Room.

Left alone, John raised Carol to her feet and held his trembling fiancée tightly in his arms. 'It's all over now, Carol,' he said. 'Nothing will ever part us again.'

A little time later the City Administrator received an urgent summons from the First Elder. Having heard of Carol's rescue and of the Engineer's capture he was worried that the Sensorite leader had discovered his complicity in the affair. As he made his way to the Palace, he considered confessing all and pleading for mercy: whatever he had done he had, after all, acted only in the best interests of the Sensorite Nation . . .

However, the First Elder had only requested his presence so that they might discuss together the serious implications of the affair and to decide what should be done to the Engineer.

'He is a menace to our society!' the Administrator declared, cleverly changing his tack. 'He must be punished and made an example to the other Sensorites!' Privately he was relieved that his servant had still remained loyal, refusing to divulge his involvement in the crime.

'He will be punished,' said the First Elder. He was pleased that his deputy was so anxious to bring the traitor to immediate justice; he was unaware of his real motives. 'But let us also find out who his accomplice is.'

'You believe there is another Sensorite working with him?' asked the Administrator, affecting, he hoped, just the right amount of incredulity.

'Obviously. He had to guard Carol. Who then delivered the letter she was forced to write?'

'She cannot identify the other Sensorite?'

'She says not.'

'It is a serious matter, sir.' The Administrator feigned concern. 'To think that a Sensorite should be capable of such a crime . . .'

'Yes . . . but what I cannot tolerate is mere accusation. Suspicions and guesses merely undermine the trust of our society. I must have clear and definite proof.'

The First Elder turned to the door as Barbara and Susan were ushered into the chamber. As they approached the First Elder they regarded the Administrator warily but kept their silence.

'You have been questioning the Sensorite Engineer who has acted so treacherously?' asked the First Elder.

'Yes,' confirmed Susan. 'And what he's told us is terrible.'

'Has he identified his accomplice yet?' The Administrator asked cautiously.

'Not yet.' Susan glared at him. It's you, isn't it, she thought, and we all know that; but the First Elder won't even contemplate the idea unless we find evidence against you. And until we do we've got to keep quiet – for our own safety.

Barbara interrupted before Susan could say anything rash. 'He did tell us however that the map and guns given to the

Doctor and Ian are useless.'

'Outrageous!' declared the First Elder. 'He will die for that.' The Administrator nodded his head in eager agreement.

'What about Grandfather and Ian though?' asked Susan.

The First Elder shrugged his shoulders. 'What can I say?' he sighed. 'Lost and unarmed in the aqueduct, they are beyond hope . . .'

Barbara clenched her fists in fury. Once again that infernal passivity, that emotionless acceptance of the facts, no matter how terrible they might be. Where was these creatures' will to fight? 'I'm afraid that answer isn't good enough,' she said firmly.

'Do not be insolent to the First Elder!' ordered the Administrator. Barbara brushed him aside.

'You must decide who your friends are and save them,' she told the First Elder, unconsciously echoing Ian's former arguments.

The First Elder stretched out his hands in a hopeless gesture. 'There is nothing I can do,' he lamented. 'You still do not understand: the noise, the dark . . .'

Barbara silently cursed the Sensorites' inadequacies. Finally she reached the only decision open to her. 'Is there another map of the aqueduct?' she asked. The First Elder said there was. 'If Susan and I find a way to rescue them will you help us?'

'I am suspicious of these creatures, sir,' whispered the Administrator, anxious that the Doctor and Ian should not be saved. 'They ask too much.'

The First Elder silenced him. 'The one called the Doctor has found a cure for the poison,' he reminded him. 'He put his life in danger for the sake of the Sensorite Nation.' He turned back to Barbara who could hardly believe that she had roused the Sensorite leader to some positive action at last. 'Yes,' he said. 'I will give you all the help I can.'

By Barbara's side Susan heaved a huge sigh of relief and gratitude.

In the dark labyrinths of the aqueduct system the Doctor and Ian's expedition had turned into a flight for their lives.

All around them, or so it seemed in the darkness, the angry growls of the Monsters of the Caves grew louder and louder. As they cautiously tried to retrace their steps down the poorly lit tunnels and back to the aqueduct entrance, threatening shadows seemed to separate themselves from the walls and follow them. They resisted the natural urge to run, knowing that if they did so they stood the chance of losing themselves in the tunnels forever.

'It seems to be getting nearer. Listen . . .' Ian remarked. If only they could see what was out there at least they would know what they were up against.

'Courage, my boy!' said the Doctor. 'Whatever's out there hasn't harmed us yet.'

For an old man at the mercy of unseen horrors, he seemed remarkably unconcerned, thought Ian, as if he knew something that he did not. No doubt he would explain in his own good time; the Doctor always did.

'Doctor, something moved slightly ahead of us,' Ian whispered, indicating a dark shadow by one of the tunnel's arches some metres ahead of them. His companion handed over the rolled-up fake map and urged him on. Carefully Ian moved forward, probing the darkness with his map, unsure of what he would find.

Suddenly the makeshift weapon was wrenched from his hand and the dark shape was upon him.

The creature knocked Ian savagely to the ground and instantly grabbed his throat. For long seconds the two stared at each other, the eyes of each of them glazed with fear and desperation. With a massive upwards lunge Ian pushed the cold clammy hands away from his throat and rolled over with his opponent in the dirt.

But the creature was far stronger than he was and once more gained the upper hand. Viciously it banged Ian's head to the ground, again and again, until it seemed to the school-teacher that it would split wide open.

The Doctor sprang to Ian's aid. Grabbing a rock from beside the pipeline he crashed it down with a massive thump onto the creature's back. For a split second it glared at the Doctor with enraged eyes and then, realising that the odds had suddenly been turned against it, it leapt to its feet and with a snarl dashed back into the darkness.

The Doctor helped the panting Ian to his feet. 'Doctor, it was a man!' Ian gasped. 'I'm sure it was!'

He showed the Doctor a strip of cloth which he had torn off the creature in the struggle. It looked like the shoulder flash of some military uniform; emblazoned in gold lettering was the word INNER.

'Just as I suspected all the time!' crowed the Doctor. 'INNER: INterstellar Navigation, Exploration and Research. He must have been one of the survivors from the spaceship that exploded!' The Doctor really was most extraordinarily pleased that his suspicions had at last been confirmed. 'Those are our Monsters, dear boy!'

'But what are they doing down here?' asked Ian.

'Why, hiding and poisoning the water of course,' the Doctor explained patiently as though he were addressing a rather dull-witted child.

'But why poison the water in the first place?' Ian continued.

'Let's go and ask him!' the Doctor said cheerily and led Ian off down the tunnel.

At the same time and unknown to the Doctor and Ian their fellow time-travellers and the First Elder were staring down at a holographic map of the very tunnels through which they were walking.

Barbara had assumed leadership of the attempt to track down and find the two men and was assailing the First Elder and his men with a barrage of questions. She needed to know the location of the aqueduct entrance, the route of the pipe-lines, and any hidden chambers or caves in which the Doctor and Ian might be able to conceal themselves from what they still believed to be the Monsters of the Caves.

'Might I be allowed to use your mind transmitter?' she asked the First Elder.

'What do you want it for?' he asked cautiously. The mind transmitter could be dangerous in the hands of a novice and he was loth to part with it unless absolutely necessary.

'John and I will go down into the aqueduct,' Barbara explained. 'Susan will stay here and guide us through the mind transmitter.'

The First Elder looked at Susan puzzledly. 'But my scientists tell me that you do not require the use of the mind transmitter.'

'I can read your minds,' Susan agreed, 'but only when you let me.'

'Your mind must be finely tuned indeed,' marvelled the Sensorites' leader. 'The frequencies covering the Sense-Sphere are numerous. You must be able to break into the major ones.'

'Well, I can't,' said Barbara. 'So do you mind if I try it?'

The First Elder reluctantly gave way. 'Very well, you have my permission,' he said and handed Barbara the small white disc. 'Try to clear your mind of everything but the person you wish to communicate with. It is safe provided that you do not let your concentration slip.'

Barbara smiled and gratefully accepted the disc. 'Susan, let's try a little experiment,' she said, placing the white disc to her forehead. Closing her eyes, Barbara attempted to send a telepathic message to the young girl.

Susan too screwed up her eyes in concentration, clearing her mind in readiness for Barbara's message.

After a few seconds Susan opened her eyes and pointed gleefully at a section of the 3D map of the aqueduct. 'The entrance to the aqueduct is – there!' she exclaimed in response to Barbara's unspoken question.

'Good, it works,' said Barbara. 'There's no point in delaying. As soon as John and I reach the aqueduct you can start directing us.' She turned to go and then considered: she had to ensure Susan's safety during her absence at all costs. 'I'd like one of your Warriors to be left here with Susan,' she said to the First Elder and then added, 'One you trust implicitly.'

'I trust *all* Sensorites,' the First Elder declared, unaware of the irony of his remark. 'She will be guarded safely.'

'Thank you.' Barbara waved her goodbyes and walked smartly out of the room. The First Elder watched her go.

'She is indeed a very capable woman: gentle yet with strong determination and courage,' he said admiringly.

Susan agreed, proud of the First Elder's assessment of her former history teacher. The pair remained in silence for a few moments and then she asked, 'Tell me, why do you trust your people so much?'

'Why do you want me to doubt them?' was the ready reply.

'Trust can't be taken for granted, even among Sensorites: it has to be earned,' Susan argued. 'I trust you but only because I know you.'

How could he make the child understand? 'Susan, our whole life is based on trust,' he said trying to make her see.

'And that might prove to be your downfall,' she warned. 'You don't trust the ground you walk on until you know it's safe, do you? So why do you trust your own people so blindly?'

The First Elder looked at the strange small girl who had, throughout their short acquaintance, constantly surprised him and raised questions and nagging doubts in his mind. 'When I listen to you who are so young among your own kind I realise that we Sensorites have a lot to learn from the people of Earth.'

Susan smiled sadly at her host's natural assumption. 'Grandfather and I don't come from Earth,' she sighed. She moved away from the First Elder and looked wistfully out of the window, past the green and blue towers of the Sensorite City, and far, far away into the twinkling night sky. There was a tone of melancholic nostalgia in her voice as she remembered her old life on the home planet, the life she had left so very long ago.

'It's ages since we've seen our planet,' she said. 'It's quite like Earth . . . but at night the sky is a burnt orange, and the leaves on the trees are bright silver . . .'

'My mind tells me that you wish to see your home again,' said the Sensorite. Susan nodded and he continued: 'Yet within you there is a part of you that calls out for adventure: a *Wanderlust* whose power cannot be stilled . . .'

Susan turned around to face the First Elder. 'Yes,' she sniffed, brushing a lone tear from her cheek. 'Still, we'll all go home someday – that is, if you'll let us . . .'

The First Elder smiled affectionately at her. 'Yes, Susan, I think I will. All of you will be able to go home.'

Deep down in the tunnel system the Doctor and Ian had been traipsing around for some time in search of Ian's attacker.

Periodically the Doctor would stop and take a piece of chalk from his pocket and make a mark on the pipe, thereby ensuring they did not lose their way.

Ian waved his torchlight around in the semi-darkness; save for the low mumbling of the water rushing through the pipes everything was quite still, a fact he pointed out to the Doctor.

'Yes, isn't it?' he chuckled. 'Just as if they're preparing an ambush!'

Ian shot his friend a look which indicated that not for the first time he was having serious doubts about his balance of mind. 'You're a cheerful soul!' he laughed.

'My boy, my spirits couldn't be higher!' the old man chortled. 'Collecting evidence, circumstantial or otherwise; evaluating information – it's all quite fascinating!'

'Doctor . . .' Ian's tone had suddenly changed to a hushed warning.

'Oh, don't interrupt me, boy. It's most irritating – ' Then the Doctor stopped, aware for the first time of the figure in front of him. Behind him he grasped Ian's hand in warning, but Ian was far more concerned with the figure in front of *him*.

They were surrounded by two men wearing INNER space uniforms. Wild-eyed with long unkempt black hair and beards, they seemed more beasts than men. They each held long sharpened clubs which they waved menacingly at the Doctor and Ian.

'You were right about the ambush, weren't you?' Ian remarked grimly.

For once the Doctor was not too pleased that he had been proved right. 'Don't do anything to alarm them,' he hissed.

As the two astronauts approached them, the Doctor and Ian slowly backed up against the pipeline. Within minutes they knew they might be dead.

12

A Desperate Venture

Up in the First Elder's chamber Carol and the Sensorite leader watched anxiously as Susan tried to contact Barbara and John. Her face was stretched in concentration as she struggled desperately to receive Barbara's thoughtwaves; but Barbara's skill at using the mind transmitter was limited and Susan could catch only a few indistinct words.

'Tell her to speak out loud to you,' suggested Carol. 'You do the same.'

Susan closed her eyes. 'Barbara, say the words as you think them,' she said, praying that Barbara would hear her clearly. Her face suddenly brightened. 'That's it!' she grinned. 'I've made contact. They're entering the aqueduct now.'

She looked down at the holographic map of the aqueduct; the route which the Doctor had taken previously was clearly marked out.

'Barbara, you're to go straight ahead to start with and then keep on turning to the right.'

Down in the aqueduct system Barbara acknowledged Susan's message and passed it on to John. They were on their way.

For what seemed an eternity no one spoke. The Doctor stared at his and Ian's two challengers with stony defiance; they returned his gaze with a look of deep suspicion. Finally one of the astronauts spoke. His voice was croaky and abrupt.

'You have come at last!' he rasped.

'We have come to find you,' the Doctor said quite truthfully.

'Watch them, Number One,' advised the other astronaut. He obviously did not trust the strangers as much as his companion did.

'We have been waiting for you,' said Number One. He cast

his eyes to the roof of the cave. 'Are they all dead up there?' he asked.

'The Sensorites, you mean?'

'Yes, the Sensorites.' He pronounced the word with distaste. 'Have you a spaceship?'

'Yes.'

'Are there more of you?'

'No.'

Number Two caught the hesitation in Ian's answer. 'No others in the channel at all?' he asked. 'You haven't brought the Sensorites with you?'

'*No!*' Ian repeated with feeling.

The Doctor calmed his companion; it would be better not to antagonise these men. 'Wouldn't you like to leave these tunnels and walk into the sunshine again?' he asked quite pleasantly.

'No. They will hear our minds.' Number One came to a decision. 'Follow me – the Commander is going to talk to you.'

'I rather thought there'd be a third,' the Doctor said to Ian.

As Number One moved off, indicating that they should follow, Number Two pushed them on their way with none too gentle prods of his spiked club.

Ian and the Doctor exchanged worried glances with each other. Whoever these men were, where ever they might be leading them, one thing was certain: they had been captured by madmen.

'How is the search progressing?' the First Elder asked Susan.

Susan opened her eyes. 'They haven't found them yet,' she said. 'But they've found Grandfather's map: Barbara says it's been tampered with. Sssh, she's trying to contact me again.'

She closed her eyes once more as Barbara's voice sounded in her head: *Susan, John's found some fresh chalk marks on the pipes. They've probably been made by the Doctor. We're going to follow them. So instead of you directing us, we'll tell you what direction we're going to take.*

'They're going down the channel now,' said Susan. She indicated their route on the map before her.

'That is strange,' remarked the First Elder. 'Perhaps the

Doctor and Ian are chasing the Monsters in the aqueducts.'

Carol feared the worst. 'Or they've been captured by them,' she said grimly.

The two astronauts had led the Doctor and Ian down a succession of winding tunnels. The roof of the narrow passageways were so low that they were forced to walk bent almost double. Ian noticed that their guides seemed to be totally at home in the tunnels and darkness, and that they moved with great speed and ease.

Finally they emerged into a large cavern, about the same size in fact as the TARDIS console room. Running along one wall of the cave was the pipeline carrying the poisoned water up into the Sensorites' City. Dotted about the cave were various shabby looking items of machinery – standard navigational and survey equipment. In the centre of this area stood a metal chest and two equipment cases which served as a makeshift table and chairs.

'Wait here,' Number One ordered his captives. He crossed over to the far wall of the cave, and called into a dark recess which obviously led into another smaller cave. 'The new arrivals are here, Commander!'

The Commander strode briskly out into the cavern. Like his two men his hair and beard had grown long over the years and his face was grey and stretched. The Doctor recognised the wild gleam of madness in his eyes and looked meaningfully at Ian: soon their fate would be decided by a lunatic.

Nothing could have prepared the two time-travellers for what happened next. A smile of pleasure broke up the Commander's careworn features and he marched over to his prisoners, his hands held out in welcome. He shook each of them vigorously by the hand. Ian and the Doctor complied in amazement, scarcely realising what was happening.

'This is the best news I've had in a long time! Good to see you both!' The Commander's voice was cultured and friendly. He could almost have been greeting old army colleagues he had not seen in years, such was his bonhomie. He looked concerned at the Doctor and Ian's grubby appearance.

'Did you have a rough journey?' he asked. 'I'm sure you must have. Please take a seat.' He showed his two bemused

133

guests to the 'chairs' and they sat down.

'Very rough quarters, I'm afraid,' he apologised, waving a hand about the cavern. 'But I'm sure you're both used to that by now. Excuse me one moment . . .'

The Commander went over to speak to Number Two and the Doctor and Ian stared at each other in bewilderment. What was going on here? Who did the Commander think they were? And more importantly, what was going to happen to them?

They listened on to the Commander's conversation with Number Two. 'You can take over ammunition detail now,' he ordered. 'Pipe the poison into Pipe Number Seven this time. Carry on!'

Number Two saluted smartly and walked briskly out of the cave. The Commander beckoned Number One to his side. 'Number One, organise a lecture for Number Two. He's been looking uncommonly untidy lately. It's not for me, you understand – it's the uniform. Is that clear?'

'Yes, sir.'

'Very good. Dismissed.'

Number One saluted and followed his colleague out of the cavern.

The Doctor had been watching and listening to this scene with fascination. Now at last all the pieces of the jigsaw had fallen into place. Forced to hide underground from the feared Sensorites, these men had been waging a secret war against the aliens, using as their only weapon the Deadly Nightshade which they had introduced into the Sensorites' water supply. They weren't evil – like all men at war they believed totally in the rightness of their mission – but they were mad, and what they were playing at was no more than an elaborate and very deadly game of soldiers.

The problem now was how to get out of these tunnels safely; the Commander had proved well disposed towards them so far but in his current mental state one ill-chosen word could turn him violently against them. He would not hesitate to kill them; in war human life could always be sacrificed for the greater good.

The Commander returned to his guests and apologised for ignoring them while he talked to his men. 'Have to keep up discipline,' he explained. 'But they're all good men. Morale's very high here.'

'You have a very well ordered base here, sir,' Ian said, humouring the man. He found it hard to disguise the pity he felt towards the Commander.

'It's very good of you to say so.' The Commander glowed with pride.

The Doctor chose his next words with care. 'I have very good news for you,' he said. 'The war with the Sensorites is over.'

The Commander could hardly believe the Doctor: this news was almost too good to be true. 'Is that so?' he asked incredulously. 'And the planet is ours now?'

'Completely,' confirmed Ian, hating himself for the cruel trick they were being forced to play on the Commander.

The Commander clapped his hands in delight. Tears of joy appeared in the corners of his eyes, but he was too much of a soldier to let them fall. 'This is absolutely wonderful!' he cried. 'We nearly lost, you know. I had command of a fine spaceship. Two of my men deserted and pretended they had to go back to Earth to get reinforcements . . .'

'So you had to blow up the craft.' The Doctor completed his sentence for him. 'Yes, well, I quite understand. You did what you had to do. In war one must make sacrifices.'

'Yes . . .' The Commander was truly saddened by what he felt he had had to do. Then his face brightened. 'Still, I suppose I can get another spaceship. I can afford it now. The planet's very rich, you know.'

'Oh yes, we do know – molybdenum,' said Ian and then wished he hadn't. Suspicion burned in the Commander's eyes.

'You know about that then, do you?' he said. 'You do realise that this war has been fought by me and my men and that any treasure trove here is ours?'

'Quite right, sir,' agreed the Doctor, hastily anxious to placate him. 'Isn't that so, Chesterton?' Ian nodded his head vigorously.

'I'm prepared to back up my statement with force if necessary,' the Commander warned. He stood to his feet and gestured about the cave. 'I have good supplies here, loyal men . . . You're hardly in a position to fight me. I have my men,' he repeated, '*and* my organisation.'

The Doctor shook his head sadly at the pathetic sight of a finely trained space officer brought down to being a broken man playing a desperate game of make-believe.

Suddenly Number One burst into the cave: 'Commander! A warning in Route Two! Intruders!'

The Commander turned viciously on the Doctor and Ian. 'Have you been telling me lies?' he demanded. 'You have brought other people down here, haven't you?'

The Doctor and Ian violently denied this; they had no idea who or what was out in the tunnels. The Commander ignored their protests.

'Perhaps they're allies of the Sensorites,' said Number One.

'No, they're spies!' barked the Commander. He grabbed the Doctor by the collar of his cloak and glared hard into his eyes. 'The war isn't over at all, is it?' he said. 'I knew it was too good to be true!'

Ian pulled the Commander's hands away from the Doctor. 'Just a minute,' he said. 'We didn't know about any warning system . . .'

'Of course you didn't!' shrieked the Commander. He addressed his deputy: 'Number One, organise a court-martial immediately!'

Onto this absurd scene of danger came suddenly the two people the Doctor and Ian least expected to see. Ian stared open-mouthed at the figures in the cave entrance. 'Barbara! John!'

The Commander turned around wildly. 'Who are these people?' he demanded to know. How could they have broken through what he believed to be a highly elaborate security system, and beaten the full might of his organisation?

The Doctor and Ian strode forwards to greet Barbara and John. There was a gentle smile on the Doctor's lips as he turned to the dumbfounded Commander. No matter how the astronaut's mind was broken he would surely see that the newcomers were not Sensorites; one was even wearing a space uniform.

'I'm afraid you've misjudged us, sir,' he said charitably.

'These people are part of the committee to welcome you. We have all come down here to take you up to the surface.'

The Commander remained puzzled until Ian added: 'To celebrate your victory over the Sensorites.'

'What's going on?' Barbara whispered to Ian. She was just as confused as the Commander.

'Play it cool,' Ian whispered back, kicking her lightly on the shin.

'Who is this?' the Commander asked, pointing at Barbara.

'She is our . . . our navigator,' explained the Doctor. 'She will lead us back.'

The Commander regarded the party with suspicion until finally John's uniform convinced him of the truth of the Doctor's words. The Commander reasoned that no member of the space corps would ever ally himself with the Sensorites.

So, the war was over at last and the Sensorites had been subdued. The battle had been hard, but his men had fought well; he would miss their companionship. It was with a touch of sadness that he finally said: 'Well, I'm glad it's all over. I'm looking forward to a bit of a rest – for a while.'

'And you and your men deserve it, sir!' agreed the Doctor. 'I dare say you'll be heralded as heroes when you get back to Earth!'

'I only did what was my duty,' said the Commander. Snapping out of his melancholy he addressed Number One who had been standing by, following the course of the conversation. 'Assemble the men – we will be leaving immediately,' he said. 'It seems we have a victory to celebrate . . . By the way, you might like to pass on my congratulations to the men.'

'Thank you very much, sir.' Number One saluted and went off to find Number Two – the only other person the Commander had to command.

As they waited for the 'men' to be assembled the Doctor looked enquiringly at Barbara who was standing by, holding in her hand the mind transmitter which would lead them back to the surface. Satisfied that Barbara was quite capable of guiding them out, he waved the rest of his party forward and brought up the rear with the Commander.

'Come along,' he said. 'The sooner we're out of these dark tunnels and back into the sunshine, the better.'

Waiting by the entrance to the aqueduct was the Senior Warrior and one of his soldiers. They were both armed. The Senior Warrior held a mind transmitter pressed to his forehead; in his mind he could hear Susan's voice directing Barbara and her small group back through the tunnels.

'They are coming,' he advised his subordinate. 'You will hide yourself out of sight behind one of the pipes. When they are all out you will step forward and prevent them going back into the aqueduct.'

The Warrior indicated his agreement and backed away. The Senior Warrior stood slightly away from the aqueduct entrance, his gun primed and ready in his hand.

Anxious minutes passed and then the Senior Warrior discerned a movement in the darkness of the tunnel. Spearheaded by Numbers One and Two the party of humans emerged from the tunnels, their eyes squinting as they accustomed themselves to the light.

The Senior Warrior stepped out in front of them. 'It is useless to resist', he warned, pointing his gun directly at the two mad astronauts who were waving their clubs about threateningly. One and Two looked despairingly back at Ian, Barbara and John, and recognised their complicity in the ambush.

The war was finally at an end. They dropped their clubs and meekly allowed themselves to be led away.

'I think John and I can handle these two,' Ian told the Senior Warrior. 'You wait for the Doctor and the other one. Lead on, Barbara.'

As Barbara took her party away, the Doctor and the Commander emerged from the tunnel entrance. The Commander instantly saw the waiting Senior Warrior and called pleadingly after his men. There was only one Sensorite: they could easily overcome it. But his men had lost the will to fight; they turned back sadly to look at their commander before disappearing through the exit and up to the surface.

The Commander moved to retreat into the tunnel but the hidden Sensorite stepped out to prevent his escape. The

Earthman looked at the Doctor with hate in his eyes. 'Treachery!' he cried.

The Doctor rested a comforting hand on his shoulder. 'It's all over now,' he said gently, aware of what the man must be going through.

'Treachery!' repeated the Commander and knocked the Doctor aside. In a final act of desperate courage he ran for the Senior Warrior. But before he could reach him a beam of invisible energy from the Sensorite's gun hit him full square in the chest. With a groan he fell senseless to the ground.

The Doctor stepped over to the Commander's prostrate form and looked down. He was still breathing. 'Pitiful fellow,' he sighed as the Senior Warrior joined him. 'I know he did your people incalculable harm – '

The Senior Warrior gently interrupted the old man. 'I could have killed him – I certainly wanted to,' he said slowly, almost wonderingly. 'But that would not have been the way, would it?'

The Doctor smiled. 'No . . .'

'He could have destroyed the entire Sensorite Nation . . .' continued the Senior Warrior.

'Yes, but the fact is you didn't kill him,' pointed out the Doctor. 'And that shows great promise for the future of your people.'

As they walked away the Doctor smiled inwardly to himself. There were those who said that he shouldn't meddle in the affairs of others, that he shouldn't become involved; at times he might be inclined to agree with them. But when his presence could generate such noble ideas in people, teach them the meaning of compassion and understanding, well, then perhaps this aimless wandering of his might have some secret purpose after all.

Several days later Barbara and Ian were in the First Elder's chamber, taking their farewells of the Sensorite leader. The First Elder had politely urged the TARDIS crew to stay for a while longer, but they had refused just as politely. All they really wanted to do was leave – and perhaps one day return to their own space and time.

'Captain Maitland has agreed to take the survivors back to

Earth,' Ian explained in answer to the First Elder's expressed concern and regret that nothing could be done for them on the Sense-Sphere.

'They were completely insane,' Barbara said. 'They really believed that they were at war with you.'

The First Elder nodded, indicating that no matter what atrocious crimes they had committed they had been forgiven: these dark days would be forever blotted from the Sensorites' history books. 'At some time they must have opened their minds or experimented with the mind transmitters,' he surmised. 'Every rational thought was crushed out and all that was left was the game they played – the game of war.'

They thought over the First Elder's words and then Barbara asked: 'What about the City Administrator – the Second Elder, I mean.'

'Your finding the altered map in his handwriting in the aqueduct proves his treachery,' said the First Elder, embarrassed that he should have been deceived for so long. 'But you should have voiced your suspicions to me.'

'Would you have listened?' asked Barbara.

'Perhaps not . . .'

'What will happen to him now?'

'His mind was warped by ambition and fear. But like the men in the caves he truly believed that what he was doing was right. He shall be banished to the Outer Wastes.'

Ian approved the First Elder's decision. 'I think we should be going back up to the ship now,' he suggested tactfully.

The First Elder granted them permission to leave. 'I shall arrange transportation,' he said. 'The others have already left for the ship. Your lock has also been returned and sealed back into its proper place.'

An awkward silence followed. Then the First Elder waved the two humans on their way.

'We have learnt much from you,' he conceded. 'Go now. And take the gratitude of the Sensorite Nation with you.'

Epilogue

Back in the TARDIS the Doctor was standing by the control console, irritably tapping his fingers together. 'Where are those other two, hmmm?' he asked Susan who was standing in a corner of the console room, idly toying with the antique astrolabe there.

'Oh, they're coming,' she said distractedly, and sauntered over to her grandfather's side. He put his arm around her, pleased that they had a few moments to themselves for once.

'What's the matter, my child?' he asked with grandfatherly concern.

'I talked to the Senior Scientists before I left,' Susan revealed. 'The Sense-Sphere has an extraordinary number of ultra high frequencies. So once I leave I won't be able to keep on using thought transference.'

Her grandfather smiled kindly at her. 'It's rather a relief, I think. After all, no one likes an eavesdropper around, do they?'

Susan smiled up gratefully at him as he continued. 'But you obviously have a gift in that direction and once we get home to our own place I think we should try to perfect it.'

'When will we get home, Grandfather?' Susan asked wistfully.

The Doctor sighed. 'I don't know, my child,' he said, his eyes seeming to look thousands of light years into the distance. 'This Ship of mine seems to be an aimless thing. However, we don't worry about that, do we? Do you?' he asked pointedly.

Susan smiled half-heartedly, remembering John and Carol's joy at being able to go home. 'Sometimes I feel I'd like to belong somewhere, not just be a wanderer,' she said, and then caught her grandfather's look of dismay. 'Still, I'm not unhappy here with you,' she added quickly.

'Good!' said the Doctor and hugged her gratefully.

As he released his granddaughter from his embrace Ian and Barbara walked through the open double doors. Embarrassed at their witnessing this show of affection, the Doctor turned on them tetchily. 'Always the last! I very nearly left without you,' he said and then operated a control on the console.

The doors closed and shortly afterwards the familiar grinding noise of dematerialisation filled the console room. The TARDIS was once more on its way through space and time.

'Let's have a look at the scanner and see Maitland off, shall we?' suggested the Doctor, operating the scanner control.

'At least *he* knows where he's going,' joked Ian, and looked up at the image of the departing spaceship on the screen. The Doctor caught the veiled criticism in Ian's quip and darted him a look which would have frozen a supernova. Resolving to teach that impertinent young man a lesson one day soon, he rejoined the others watching Maitland's departure on the screen.

As Maitland's ship sailed further away only Barbara stood apart from her companions and watched the TARDIS scanner with some misgiving.

Maitland, Carol and John were good people and would guard the Sensorites' secret well. But she remembered other instances in Earth's history when promises had been made and then broken; when secrets had been kept and later betrayed. She remembered the dreadful consequences of such actions: the callous exploitation of the Indians of North America, the Aborigines of Australia. In their own naive way the Sensorites were just as helpless as them.

For the moment the Sensorites were safe, their security and well-being in the stewardship of Maitland, Carol and John. But what of the future?

There would be questions asked, investigations carried out. The Earth authorities would want to know the circumstances behind the temporary disappearance of Maitland's ship. Could the Sense-Sphere and its priceless molybdenum remain a secret forever?

Rich beyond the dreams of avarice, John had said. Throughout human history men had given in to the lure of greed, though they justified it with words like progress, development, expansion, and conveniently forgot things like morality, fairness and compassion. Had human nature then changed so much?

She dismissed the thought from her mind and joined her friends. She was being a silly old worrier. Perhaps in the twenty-eighth century mankind had grown up. Perhaps this time it would be different.